LAKEHOUSE PROMISES

JODI ALLEN BRICE

CHAPTER 1

"*H*urry up or we'll be late."

Carolina Johnson took one last glimpse at her reflection in the bathroom mirror and turned her face side-to-side, checking for any signs of misplaced makeup. She'd chosen the stylish cream-colored blouse with the billowy sleeves and paired it with her dark jeans, hoping to hide her stomach.

She cast a longing look at her ballet flats but knew the other ladies would be wearing heels at the party.

She sighed and slipped her feet into the nude-colored high heels before hurrying into the kitchen where her husband, Chris, was waiting.

"How do I look?"

"You look fine. We need to get these over to the Barker's before everyone else arrives." He shoved the platter of hors d'oeuvres she'd made that afternoon into her arms.

She frowned. "You're wearing swim trunks and a T-shirt."

He shrugged, slightly irritated. "Yeah. It's a pool party."

"Do I need to get my swimsuit?" Just the thought made her stomach turn.

"No, no. I'm sure it's just the men getting in the pool. Don't worry about it." He grabbed his cooler of iced beer and headed out to the garage.

Carolina stuck the hostess gift under her arm and managed to gingerly walk down the steps to the garage while balancing the food tray in her hands.

The garage door was up and Chris was sitting in the driver's seat tapping his fingers on the steering wheel impatiently. She ignored his impatient look and managed to open the door with her free hand and get in without spilling the hors d'oeuvres or dropping the gift.

She was already tired and hadn't even left the house.

Parties used to be fun and relaxing, but they had quickly morphed into opportunities for everyone to show off a new outfit or piece of jewelry.

The ride over to the Barker's was quick and quiet and she was grateful. Lately Chris had been in a foul mood and everything she said seemed to upset him.

When they arrived at their destination her husband pulled into the driveway and killed the engine. One of the other husbands waved. Chris quickly got out of the car and headed over to speak to the guy without offering to help her with the appetizers. A few seconds into the conversation, they were drinking beer and Carolina was quickly forgotten.

"Perfect." She muttered and finagled her way out of the car, a feat in and of itself, given the platter she still held in her hands. Teetering on high heels, she made her way up the steps. She peered through the glass of the front door but didn't see anyone. Leaning against the door for balance, she managed to press her thumb against the doorbell.

A rich tune emanated from the other side. A few seconds passed before the door opened.

"Carolina! Hello. So glad you could make it." Lydia Barker smiled and waved her inside.

"Thanks for the invitation, Lydia. It's been a while since we've gotten together." Carolina followed her into the kitchen and set the tray down on the counter. She handed her the hostess gift tucked in the crook of her arm. "This is for you."

"Oh, how lovely. Thank you." Lydia peered inside the bag and pulled out an expensive candle. "My favorite scent. How very thoughtful of you."

"You're welcome." Carolina relaxed a little. She'd taken a long time in the boutique trying to decide on a scent. She usually liked basic scents like vanilla and peach. After twenty minutes of indecision, she finally went with the salesperson's suggestion and picked the most popular one.

Carolina glanced around and spotted a few familiar faces around the room. No matter how many times she met someone, she was always afraid they wouldn't remember her. Like she wasn't memorable, quite unlike her husband, Chris, who easily made friends where ever he went.

"Carolina, you remember Jackie, don't you?" Lydia smiled at the tall, buxom, brunette with the perfect figure. Her body was wrapped in a stunning red dress, a garment so tight, it looked like it had been melted onto her shapely figure.

"Of course. How are you, Jackie? You are looking great." Carolina smiled brightly, as she wrapped a self-conscious hand around her not-slim-enough waist.

"Thank you. I just got back from a trip to the beach. Let me tell you a tan always makes you look slimmer." She ran her hand down her waist. "What kind of vacations have you been on?"

Carolina laughed. "None, I'm afraid. Chris has been much too busy at work to book any vacations this year."

Jackie arched her brow. Her lips pressed together in a thin line that caused Carolina's stomach to tilt a little.

"I'm sure we'll do something soon though," she added quickly, not wanting Jackie to think she was weird for not taking a vacation. It was almost October and all their friends and families had taken at least two vacations this year. That didn't even include all the holiday trips they usually planned.

"Robin!" Jackie waved to someone across the room and made her way over, leaving Carolina standing there alone.

Carolina quickly searched the room for a familiar face. Her gaze landed on Audrey. She picked up a glass of wine and made her way over.

"Audrey, hi." She smiled brightly.

"Carolina." Audrey's smile slid off her face and she glanced out the doors that led to the swimming pool. "I didn't know you were here."

"Yes, sorry we're a little late. Seems like a good turnout for a party." Carolina looked around.

"Look, I don't think you should be here." Audrey's expression hardened.

Carolina blinked. Surely she'd not heard correctly. "I'm sorry, it sounded like you said…"

"Carolina, you really shouldn't be here." Audrey cast a nervous glance out the window. Her face went pale. Without a word she quickly stood up and took Carolina by the arm, urging her toward the door.

Carolina's body felt like marble. She couldn't move and felt heavier than her normal pudgy self. Humiliated, her eyes stung with unshed tears. She wanted to sink into the floor, beneath the rich earth where no one could see her.

"You're hurting me," Carolina whispered, hoping no one was watching.

"I'm trying to help you." Audrey hissed.

At that moment, Chris burst into the room with a young woman dressed in a scantily clad black dress and high heels. She grabbed Chris's arm, reached up on her tiptoes, and kissed him square on the mouth.

Carolina couldn't move. She couldn't trust her eyes.

5

Surely she was hallucinating. Her legs went weak and she feared she might actually pass out. Dear Lord, did she have a brain tumor?

"Kylie, stop." Chris gently shoved the woman back, his face red with embarrassment.

"But this is great news, sweetheart. We're going to have a baby." The perfect specimen of a woman, who was everything Carolina was not, twirled in his arms.

Good Lord, now she was having audible hallucinations. Was it early dementia? Psychosis? Was she schizophrenic?

Just then, as if Kylie sensed Carolina's presence, she turned and their eyes met. She was beautiful, thin, young, with a perfect body. "You must be the old wife. I'm Kylie, the soon-to-be new wife."

Carolina reached for Audrey's arm. "Something's wrong with me, Audrey. I think I need a doctor."

The next thing she remembered of that horrid night, was Audrey's breath on her ear as her words rang out in her muddled head. "No sweetie. You don't need a doctor. You need a lawyer."

"rs. Johnson, do you understand everything I've read to you?"

Carolina blinked and tried to concentrate on what John Rithers, her attorney, was saying.

"The judge is awarding you alimony for three years, unless you remarry before that time, then you forfeit any alimony."

"I won't be getting married again." Carolina pressed her hand to her stomach.

"And your husband gets the house." John shook his head. "I don't like it. The judge should have ruled that Chris should sell the house and split the proceeds."

"He won't sell. That's his dream house. He had everything custom-built." She wanted to lay down and go to sleep for a week.

Since discovering her husband's affair, she hadn't slept, nor had she eaten. Minutes had bled into days which seeped into weeks.

She'd cried and begged Chris not to throw away their marriage for someone he hardly knew.

But it had been clear from the way he stared blankly into her eyes that he had already made his choice.

He had chosen Kylie.

"Carolina, the judge did award you the lake house. Once you agree and sign the terms, you will be responsible for the upkeep of the house. Do you understand?" He cocked his head and waited for her reply.

She nodded.

"Can I get you some more coffee?"

She rubbed her temple. "No thank you. Anymore and I'll be sick to my stomach."

"Per the settlement agreement, you have one day to get your stuff out of the house. There will be a police officer who will be there with you just in case there are any issues."

"A police officer?"

"Yes. Just to make sure nothing goes wrong. You'll be given an hour to get your clothing."

"That's it? Just my clothing? What about my pictures?"

He gave her a look of sympathy. "Do you really want any of those?"

She shrugged. Unshed tears stung the back of her eyes.

"What about my car?"

"You will keep the Jeep Grand Cherokee."

"That's Chris's vehicle. He bought it when he

thought he wanted to start hunting again." She frowned. "What about my Mercedes?"

"Chris pays the lease on the Mercedes so the judge said he could keep it." He reached over and patted her hand. "Remember, the Jeep is paid off. Right now, you need to focus on reducing your expenses until you can get back on your feet and get a job."

A job. She'd not worked in the twenty years since she married Chris. Who was going to hire a forty-year-old divorcee with no experience?

She nodded and reached inside her purse for a Kleenex. She pulled it out and realized even though her eyes stung, she had no more tears to shed.

"Carolina, do you understand everything I've told you? It's a lot to take in," he asked gently.

"Yes, I think so. When can I go to my house to get my things?"

"I can arrange it today if you want?"

She nodded and nervously tore the Kleenex into tiny bits.

"I can go with you if you wish," he offered.

"No. I'll be okay. You said an officer will be there?"

"Yes. Here are the keys to the Jeep." He slid them across the desk to her.

She wrapped her fingers around the cold keys. "I need to get this over with." She stood and walked over to the window and looked out wondering how she would survive her bleak future.

CHAPTER 3

Carolina sat parked outside in the musty smelling Jeep. She was told to wait until the police officer arrived before entering the house.

She glanced at the orange and yellow mums in her flowerbed.

She had planted those last fall and had looked forward to enjoying them when Thanksgiving came around. Sadly she wouldn't get to enjoy them this year, or any year after.

When the divorce started, the judge had ordered that Chris stay somewhere else while she stayed in the home. Three days ago, the judge had amended the order and directed her to stay at a hotel until a final ruling was issued. She didn't realize at the time that she had stayed in her home for the last time. She had seen other couples divorce and the wife always got the house. So when the final ruling came down she had been shocked.

Movement at the window caught her attention.

She squinted to make out who it was.

Kylie.

Anger immediately replaced grief as she reached for the door handle.

She stepped out into the October wind and wrapped her arms around herself from the elements. The overcast sky had opened up and started to sprinkle. As she made a dash to the door, cold drops of rain soaked into her sweater. Why hadn't she thought to bring a coat this morning?

She didn't look at the weather forecast anymore.

She could barely remember what day it was.

With anger boiling in her veins, she stomped toward the front door, keeping her eyes on Kylie standing at the window.

She reached for the door handle and turned, but it was locked.

Puzzled she removed the key from her purse and inserted it into the tiny hole.

She turned the knob. Nothing.

She tried again, this time using more force. Again, nothing.

Then it dawned on her. The little witch inside had bolted the door from the inside, leaving her unable to enter.

Her anger hit a new level.

She pounded her fist against the door. Kylie did not move. She stood glaring at her through the door with a smirk on her face.

The blast of sirens had her turning around.

A young police officer got out of the patrol car and hurried up to her. "Ma'am, you're not supposed to go in without a police escort."

"What is she doing in my house?" She jerked her thumb at Kylie's smirking face. "No one is supposed to be here while I'm packing my things."

The police officer knocked once on the door. Kylie promptly opened it.

"Yes, officer?" She gave him an innocent smile.

"Ma'am. Are you the resident of the house?"

"Yes I am."

"No, she's not." Carolina glared. "The house belongs to my husband..er, my ex-husband."

The officer glanced between them, then turned his attention on Kylie. "What's your name, ma'am?" The police officer addressed Kylie.

"Kylie Johnson." She smiled and held out her hand.

Carolina's stomach dropped when she spotted the large diamond ring and matching wedding band on the twenty-year-old's bony hand.

"He married you?" The words rushed out of Carolina's mouth before she could stop them.

Kylie smirked."This morning. After your divorce was final. We went to the courthouse." She placed her hands on her growing baby bump. "Of course, we will have a large wedding ceremony once the baby is here and I can fit into my dream dress."

Carolina felt the nausea march up the back of her throat. White spots danced in front of her eyes.

"Ma'am. Are you okay?" The officer, seeing her face, touched her arm gently.

"Where is Chris?" Carolina asked softly.

"He's running errands." Kylie shrugged as she admired her ring.

So he couldn't even face her with the news he'd immediately remarried. He took the coward's way out.

"Ma'am? Do you want to come back another day to get your things?" The police officer studied her face. "Perhaps another time would be better… for everyone involved."

She shook her head. She would not be coming back here. Not ever again.

"No. I want to do it now." She lifted her head and pointed. "My bedroom is this way."

The police officer turned to Kylie, "Why don't you go into the kitchen while she gathers her things?"

"What if she takes something that belongs to me?" Kylie glared.

"I don't want anything that belongs to you." Carolina headed to the bedroom.

When she reached what had once been her bedroom, she opened the door and stood there, shocked. The unmade bed had different bedding on it. Instead of the soft gray and white comforter, there was a brightly colored polka dot comforter that looked like it belonged on a child's bed.

Her beautiful gray walls had been painted over with a turquoise blue and all the pictures on the wall had been taken down and replaced with weird artwork.

On top of those changes, the normally neat room was messy. The drawers on the new dresser were open with undergarments hanging out, and clothes were strewn on the floor.

Carolina took in a deep breath and tamped down her anger while she headed to the large walk-in closet.

She opened the doors and immediately froze.

All her clothing had been taken off the hangers and thrown into a pile on the floor. Kylie had already made herself at home and put her clothes up where Carolina's once hung.

She pulled down a suitcase from the top shelf and unzipped it.

Kylie appeared in the doorway. "Nope. She doesn't get the suitcase."

"It's my suitcase." Carolina stood her ground.

Kylie produced a piece of paper. "According to the judge's orders she can take her clothes and that's it." She shoved the document at the police officer.

He narrowed his eyes and took the sheet. After reading it, he handed it back to Kylie.

With an apologetic expression he turned to Carolina. "I'm afraid she's right."

Carolina grabbed up a pile in her arms and started for the door.

"Once she leaves she can't come back and get the rest." Kylie smirked and waved the court document in the air.

"How can I get all my clothes if I don't have something to put them in?" Carolina asked.

"Not my problem." Kylie crossed her arms over her large belly.

Carolina blinked. She'd hit rock bottom and now, on top of everything she'd endured, she was being completely humiliated.

Her jaw stiffened. "Where are the old sheets that were on the bed?"

"In the laundry room. In the pile for the maid to throw out when she comes and cleans."

"You have a maid?" Carolina blinked.

"Of course. Chris can't expect me to keep house and be pregnant." She smirked.

She was stunned. Carolina had always kept the house spotless, ran errands, kept the laundry up, and managed to work in the flower beds. When Chris's difficult mom had moved in with them last year after hip surgery, Carolina had brought up the subject of getting a maid. Chris shot her down.

Yet he had given in with Kylie.

Carolina marched past Kylie to the laundry room. She found the old sheet set wadded up in the corner.

She carried them back into the closet where she spread out the fitted sheet and began piling all her clothes in the middle. When it was full she grabbed all four corners and tied them together. She spotted her shoes and began throwing them into the two pillow-cases. She went to where her jewelry box was and stopped.

"Where's my jewelry box?"

"I don't know what you mean." Kylie arched her

brow.

"There was a box on this shelf. It contained all my jewelry that my mother left me before she died."

Kylie shrugged.

Carolina looked at the police officer.

"If you want, you can file a police report for theft," he said.

Kylie shifted her weight.

"I think I'd like to do that." Carolina kept her eyes on Kylie, daring her to push any further.

The officer nodded. He pulled out a pen from his front shirt pocket and began writing on the clipboard he held.

"Wait! Why don't I talk to Chris first? He might have misplaced it," Kylie said a little too quickly.

The police officer glanced at his watch. "Is there anything else you need to get?"

Carolina drew a deep breath. "Can I walk through the house?"

"I don't think that's a good idea." Kylie spoke up.

Carolina looked at the officer.

"According to the document, she has a right to walk through the house and collect her belongings." He looked at Kylie.

Satisfied Carolina carried her bundle of clothes to the front door. She wiped her hands on her thighs feeling the turn of her wedding band.

She walked through the house room by room, noting that every sign of her ever having lived there had been erased.

Any photos of her had been taken down. Her favorite blanket which laid on the back of the couch in the living room had been removed. Her Bible, which was on the coffee table was gone.

"Where's my Bible?" She turned to the officer, giving him a pleading look. "My Bible is gone."

Kylie suddenly appeared and went to a cabinet underneath the bookcase. She pulled out the missing Bible and shoved it at Carolina's chest.

Thankfully she wrapped her hands around it and held it to her chest.

"Anything else ma'am? You're almost out of time."

"Yes. My mother's quilt. It was in the guest bedroom. It's gone."

Kylie crossed her arms over her chest. "We threw it away. It didn't fit our décor."

Tears stung Carolina's eyes. "Why would you do that? It was the last thing she gave me before she died."

"I'm sorry ma'am. Maybe it's best for everybody if you finish up as quickly as possible."

Tears slid down her face. While the court order stated she had time to collect her things, she didn't have it in her to argue anymore.

Clasping the Bible to her chest she trudged to the door, where she shoved the Bible in the pillowcase with her shoes and grabbed her meager belongings.

As she trudged to the jeep in the misting rain, she noticed her neighbors across the street staring at her from their open garage.

It was the perfect ending to a horrible day.

CHAPTER 4

The rain had gone from a drizzle to a downpour. After driving out of her neighborhood, Carolina blinked back tears at a life she was leaving behind. She tapped her thumbs against the steering wheel, waiting for the stoplight to turn. When the light flashed green, Carolina turned onto the street that went to the bank to settle things there. She had to open a new account and then send the information and account number to her attorney, so he could tell Chris where to deposit the alimony check.

Within a matter of weeks, her life had gone from financially charmed, to almost destitute.

Her stomach growled, but she ignored it. If she wanted to get to the lake house before dark she needed to get on the road. Besides if she ate right now it would probably come right back up.

The fierceness of the rain beat against the windshield and slowed her drive to the lake house.

She really didn't mind. She wasn't in a hurry. Once she got there she didn't know what she would do. Her whole life had circled around being a wife. Now that she wasn't, she wasn't sure of her purpose.

Actually she was a little surprised that Chris had given her the lake house in the divorce.

They'd bought the house seven years ago on a small lake in North Carolina. When they first bought the house, she expected to be at the lake every weekend, but after a few months Chris said he didn't like driving three hours to get there, so he ended up renting it out. The lake house stayed pretty booked up because every time Carolina wanted to go to the lake, he said it was rented.

She glanced at the time on her phone. According to Google maps, she was fifteen minutes away from the lake house. She finally pulled into the small town of Hopeton and knew she needed to at least stop and pick up something for dinner before it got too late. She spotted a grocery store and parked. Grabbing her keys and her purse she headed out into the rain.

The grocery store was a mom-and-pop shop with only one freezer section and a small bakery area. She grabbed a shopping cart and quickly found coffee and some milk for the morning. She added a loaf of bread and some deli meat for a quick dinner. She grabbed a case of water and some cans of soup, and added those to the cart as well. She tossed in some toothpaste, soap, shampoo, and conditioner. She had no idea if there was laundry detergent so she threw that in.

If she needed more supplies she would just drive back into town tomorrow.

She headed to the register and unloaded her cart.

The elderly woman behind the counter smiled and began ringing up her supplies.

"How are you today, dear?"

"Okay." The words came out automatically.

She lied. She wasn't okay. Not by a long shot.

"Are you visiting?"

"No. I'm headed to my lake house." She spotted a novel on the shelf and added that to her items.

"How lovely. For a visit?" She aimed the scan bar at the case of water.

"No. To live. My divorce was final today and I got the lake house. He got everything else."

"Oh I'm so sorry." Her expression shifted to sympathy. "My name is Dee. I own the grocery store with my husband, Lawrence." She continued her task of checking out the grocery items while filling Carolina in on the town and its residents. Carolina thought the woman knew an awful lot about everybody and everybody's business.

"Now what did you say your name was, honey?"

"I'm Carolina Johnson." She forced a smile.

Dee's smile slid off her face. "Did you say Johnson?"

"Yes."

"You own the lake house in the cove?"

"Yes. Do you know it?"

She let out a little huff. "I know the cops have been called on the people who rented it out last month."

Carolina jerked her head up. "What?"

"Yes. They were disturbing the neighbors and they had a vicious dog that attacked someone."

Her hand went to her mouth. "I had no idea. My husband managed the rental property and dealt with any issues."

Dee finished bagging up her items and gave her a sympathetic look. "I'm afraid your neighbors might not be too happy when they find out the owner is moving in. I'm pretty sure those folks have a lot to say about the unfortunate incident. I mean, these people were hopping mad. Especially after multiple attempts to reach your husband. I hear he didn't bother to return any of their calls."

"My ex-husband." Carolina reminded her. "It's not my fault. I had no idea."

"Just be careful and keep the noise down. Maybe everyone's forgotten all about it." She patted her hand. "Oh and welcome to town."

CHAPTER 5

Carolina had a difficult time finding the lake house. The last time she'd been there had been years ago. She almost missed the driveway because it was overgrown and it was hard to see in the dark.

She slowly drove up the driveway and frowned. They'd paid a grounds crew to keep up the yard which included the driveway. Even though it was fall they should have continued to keep up the yard, yet it looked like no one had taken care of the place for months.

Her headlights hit the front of the house and her foot hit the brakes. She peered through the windshield, horrified at what she saw.

The house's red paint was peeling and in desperate need of a fresh paint job. The flowerbeds were over-grown with weeds and grass and all her perennial flowers had long since died.

So, this is why Chris let her have the place. He knew it was a wreck. Undoubtedly, getting the house back in shape would cost several thousand dollars—money she simply didn't have.

Carolina took a steady breath, trying to calm her racing heart.

What she needed was some dinner and a good night's sleep. Everything would look better in the morning, she reminded herself.

She killed the engine and opened the door of the jeep. She pulled out her bag of groceries and one of the sheets filled with her clothes. She set her items by the door. She made two more trips in the rain.

Fishing the house keys out of her purse, she unlocked the large door and pushed it open.

The scent of mildew assaulted her senses.

She sat her sheets filled with her clothes on the floor and reached for the light switch.

The light flickered before illuminating the foyer.

The small table she'd bought for the entryway was gone. And so was the runner.

The hardwood floors were scratched and dull. They definitely needed to be sanded and refinished.

She headed further into the house. The living room opened up into the kitchen.

The large picture window that looked out over the lake had sold them on the property. The view was stunning. She had pictured Christmases at the lake house but that had never happened. Chris preferred to have Christmas at home.

The stone fireplace looked to be in good shape but the mantle needed dusting and the TV was missing from where it hung above.

She looked around the kitchen and noticed the sink dripping. Walking over she turned the faucet but the drip continued.

The living room couch and coffee table had stains on them.

She frowned.

Chris had not told her about any damage from renters they'd had.

She shook her head.

No wonder he let her have the lake house.

Her stomach growled and she headed back to the front door to grab her groceries.

She picked up her bags and the bottom felt wet against her arm. She glanced inside to see if her soup cans had busted.

A deep sense of dread settled in her stomach.

The inside was dry. She glanced over at the sheet holding her clothes and noticed a dark ring around the bottom. Reaching down, she touched it.

She pressed her hand to the ground. It was wet.

Horrified she looked up at the ceiling.

That's when she noticed the large wet ring on the ceiling.

"How long has it been like that?" She muttered to herself.

She stood and rubbed her hand to her temple.

Another headache was brewing and she couldn't really think right now.

She grabbed the biggest pot out of the kitchen and put it under the leak.

Then she took her clothes into the laundry room. She turned on the light and realized the dryer was gone.

Her stomach began to hurt. Could things get any worse?

She made a mental note to call her attorney tomorrow and ask him why she had not been informed of all the damage to the lake house.

Right now, it was late and there was nothing she could do.

She sat her pile of clothes on the washing machine.

Without a dryer there was no use in washing her clothes tonight.

She walked back into the kitchen and opened a cabinet. All the red dishes she'd bought for the lake house were gone. She opened the next cabinet thinking the renters had just moved some items around.

The coffee cups were gone except for a large mug whose handle was broken off.

Her silverware was gone, replaced with a set of plastic utensils.

She sighed. Her hunger was now gone, replaced by an overwhelming tiredness she felt deep inside.

Thankfully the coffeepot was still there. It was a cheap one she'd picked up at a yard sale. She didn't find any filters but did find some paper towels. She fashioned a homemade filter, prepped the coffee for the morning and set the timer.

She headed into the master bedroom, trying to brace herself for what she might find there.

She flipped the light switch and looked around.

The furniture was gone. The only thing left was a stained mattress on the floor that had seen better days.

She went down the hall into the other two bedrooms. One still had the furniture but was missing the mattress. And the other bedroom had nothing.

Her shoulders sagged and she felt like she couldn't catch her breath. She blinked back the tears which stung her eyes.

So much for a good night's sleep. She wondered if she would ever have a moment in her new life when she didn't feel so overwhelmed with fear.

Swallowing down the pain in her heart, she walked out of the room.

In the living room she stood at the window and looked out. Tiny dots of lights from the other houses lit up around the lake.

It looked serene from where she stood.

Shaking her head she grabbed her purse and headed out the front door. She locked it and went to her car. She slid into the driver's seat and contemplated driving back into town to get a hotel for the night.

It was a short distance, but she could barely hold her eyes open.

Resting her head back on the seat she closed her eyes and prayed tomorrow would be better.

a knock on her window had her bolting upright in her seat.

"Ouch." She winced at the sharp pain in her neck reminding her she was no spring chicken and clearly had no business sleeping in a car.

It was early dawn and light was just starting to break.

"Hello?"

She turned to the person standing outside her car window.

She reached for the button but remembered the windows were manual. Slowly cranking the handle she let the window down enough to speak to the stranger on the other side wearing a hooded coat.

"You can't sleep here. This is private property." Stern eyes stared at her from the hood.

"Oh, I'm not trespassing. I'm the owner." She smiled bleakly, hoping for a dab of friendliness.

The figure shoved their hood down and, for the first time, Carolina realized the person outside her window was a woman.

The lady stepped back and Carolina scrambled out of the car. The cold wind cut through her like a knife. She wrapped her arms around herself.

"If you're the owner why are you sleeping out here?" She cocked her head like she didn't believe her.

"Well, I got in late last night. And realized…" She swallowed. How much should she be telling this woman?

"I'm sorry. I didn't introduce myself. I'm Carolina Johnson." She stuck out her hand.

"I'm Bernice Stacks. I live three houses down." She didn't take her hand but pointed in the direction of her home.

Carolina forced a bright smile. "Nice to meet you."

Bernice narrowed her eyes. "I've never actually met the owner of this house."

"Yeah, when we bought it we intended to spend weekends here. Unfortunately, my husband was on call a lot…" She swallowed hard. "I mean my ex-husband."

"So, you're divorced?" Her eyebrows shot up.

"As of yesterday, yes." She wrapped her arms tighter around herself.

"I see. Mrs. Johnson, did your ex-husband keep you apprised of the goings on here on the lake?"

"No." She frowned. "He said it would be a better option to rent it out since we couldn't make it out here every weekend. Why? Is there a problem?" Her stomach dropped.

"You bet there's a problem." Bernice glared. "The last few months *your* house was rented to a bunch of troublemakers. There were parties every night. One of the neighbor's mailboxes was knocked down by one of them while they were driving drunk, and their dog attacked Mrs. Phillips' weiner dog and it had to have surgery."

Carolina gasped. "Oh my gosh. I had no idea…"

"And the police were called multiple times." Bernice crossed her arms over her chest and huffed.

Nausea rolled in Carolina's stomach. White stars flashed before her eyes.

"Are you okay?" Bernice leaned in. "You don't look so good."

"I'm just." She leaned against the car for support. "I didn't eat yesterday. I just need some coffee." She blinked away the stars in her vision and started for the house. Suddenly the cold air felt good against her skin.

"Wait.." Bernice called after her but it was like white noise in Carolina's ears.

She had to keep walking. She had to escape while she could.

She quickly unlocked the front door and stepped inside.

The water in the pot had grown deeper, but she couldn't worry about that right now. She needed to sit down first.

She collapsed on the couch and thought she saw a cloud of dust rise out of the cushions.

She put her head in her hands and took some deep breaths. Her vision slowly cleared.

She smelled the familiar and very welcoming aroma of freshly-made coffee. Her spirits lifted slightly. Thankfully she'd had the coffee set before she went to sleep last night. It was a habit she had yet to break.

She stood and walked into the kitchen to fix a cup of coffee in the broken mug.

Adding some milk to the coffee she went out onto the back deck. Leaves were scattered about but the wrought iron furniture looked to be in good shape. She scraped some leaves off an orange cushion and settled into the chair.

Sipping on her coffee she tried to force her mind to go blank. For once she didn't want to think about her problems and her future. She just wanted to be okay.

She closed her eyes and sat in the silence until the cold was too much to bear.

Shivering, she went back inside and looked for her phone.

She dialed her attorney's office and was immediately put on hold. When the secretary, Jennifer, came back on, Carolina explained her situation with the lake house. The secretary assured her that she would pass on the information once her attorney was back in the office after court.

Feeling a bit defeated, Carolina slumped down on the dusty couch and sighed.

The house smelled.

She lifted her arm and sniffed.

She smelled too.

She stood and wandered into the bathroom. In the tiny linen closet she found some towels and washcloths but they were pretty worn out. She also found a half-used bottle of shampoo underneath the sink and a sliver of soap.

First things first.

She needed to shower and get a fresh change of clothes on.

Carolina headed out to her car and brought in the rest of her things stuffed in pillowcases and sheets.

She quickly pulled out some jeans, sneakers, and a long sleeve T-shirt. She left her phone on the bathroom sink and turned the volume all the way up in case her attorney called while she was in the shower.

Turning on the faucet, she made sure the water was hot before jumping in. When the temperature was right, she got in and let the water run over her while she attempted to scrub her troubles away.

By the time she got out, the water was cold.

She quickly toweled off and dressed.

She found a hair dryer in the drawer and plugged it in. She turned it on and aimed it at her head. It made a few grinding noises before blowing out some smelly blue sparks.

She quickly unplugged it and threw it in the garbage can and then waved her hand in the air to disburse the smoke.

Could anything else go wrong?

She towel-dried her short brown hair the best she could and slipped on her tennis shoes.

Finding her purse she dug out a pen and a scrap of paper. She wrote down a list of basic toiletry supplies and added a new hair dryer as well.

She hadn't seen any cleaning supplies so she added that to the list.

Her phone rang just as she was jotting down kitchen supplies.

"Hello?"

"Carolina, Jennifer said you called. She explained that things at the lake house aren't like you had expected."

"No, they're not," she admitted, trying to use a firm demeanor. This was no time to waiver. He needed to know just how bad it was. She'd been given the shaft and her attorney needed to make things right some-how. She cleared her throat and went on, " Most of the bedroom furniture is missing and there's a leak in the roof that's dripping into my foyer. No one has tended to the landscaping in months. The house needs painting inside and out and my TV, dryer, and dishes are gone. I had to sleep in my car last night, and was awakened by an angry neighbor who informed me there had been some trouble from the last renters who apparently ran over a someone's mailbox, and got so loud that the cops were called.

"Hmmm. Chris didn't disclose that in the docu-ments when I asked about the lake house. He said everything had been kept up and was in good working order."

"This place is far from good working order. What am I supposed to do? I can't live in it like it is."

"Can you stay at a hotel while I get this sorted out?"

"I guess."

"I'll get back to you as soon as I can. Court is about to be in session and I've got to go."

She stared at the phone after he had hung up.

When she finally stood she went to the laundry room and angrily grabbed her wet clothes. Hopefully the hotel would have a laundry service.

Of course, given her streak of luck, she'd have to wash her items in the lake and hang them on the trees to dry.

Sticking all her belongings in the back of the jeep she climbed into the driver's seat and started the engine.

CHAPTER 7

*C*arolina pulled into the small town of Hopeton and followed the signs for the hotel. She pulled into the front of the rustic-looking Hopeton Motel and grabbed her purse.

She remembered staying at the motel on vacation with her mom and dad when she was little.

The place didn't seem as charming and cute now as it did back then.

She took a deep breath and made her way to the entrance and opened the door to the office.

Inside, an older man sat on a stool behind the counter, wearing a fishing hat decorated with fishing lures, folded his paper down and looked at her over his glasses. "Can I help you?"

"Yes. I would like a room."

He cocked his head. "You're not on the run, are you?"

"Of course not. She patted down her damp hair and

gasped. "Why would you say that?"

"Because we don't get many single women checking in. Mostly families or couples."

"It's just me." She twisted the band on her finger.

His gaze landed on her finger.

"I'm divorced," she quickly explained.

He looked down at his ledger and flipped a page.

"I have room twelve available. But it won't be ready until one."

"I'll take it." She fished in her purse for a credit card and slid it across the desk to him.

"In the meantime, can you point me in the direction of a laundromat?"

"Sure. If you take a right off this street you'll see Clean As A Whistle Laundromat at the end of the block." He typed the information from her credit card into a dated looking computer.

"Thanks." She glanced around the wood-paneled room. There was a small kitchenette set up along the wall with some pastries and what looked like a pot of hot oatmeal.

Her stomach growled reminding her she needed to get something to eat soon.

"How long were you planning to stay?" He looked up at her.

"I'm not sure." She froze. All her life she'd let Chris make the big decisions when it came to fixing things around the house. How long would it take for someone to fix the leak in the roof? A week? A month? Longer?

"I should warn you, I only have two nights available

right now. We have a group for a class reunion and they have rented a large block of rooms for a week."

She sighed. "Then I'll take the two nights."

He nodded and slid a room key across the counter to her. "The room should be ready at one. Maybe a little sooner."

"No rush. I'm headed to get breakfast and then do some shopping." She frowned. "I didn't see a large retail store when I drove in. Is there a Target or Walmart close by?"

"We have Harry's Marketplace out by the highway. But if you are looking for some antiquing check out Maggie's Treasures. It's on the same street as the laundromat. You can't miss it."

"Thank you." She stuck her key and credit card back in her purse.

Walking outside she noticed how bright the sky looked. That was good news for her roof. At least it wouldn't get any wetter in her house.

She climbed back in her car and headed in the direction of the laundromat. She spotted a small café on the same block.

Her need for sustenance won out over the need for clean clothes.

She pulled into an empty parking spot in front. She noticed the small restaurant was almost full of patrons.

That was a good sign.

She opened the door and a bell tinkled overhead. A few of the customers sitting at the counter turned to see who it was.

A passing waitress smiled. "Just sit anywhere, honey. I'll be with you in a minute."

Carolina nodded and found an empty spot at the end of the counter.

Another waitress placed a cup in front of her and filled it with coffee. She was older and wore a smile like most wore jewelry. Her general demeanor made her sparkle.

"Special today is two eggs, bacon, hash browns, and toast for five ninety-nine."

Carolina's stomach rumbled. "I'll take it." She doctored her coffee with cream and sugar while the waitress wrote her order down and then gave it to the cook through a tiny window leading into the kitchen.

The hum of voices seemed to soothe her frazzled mind as she drank her coffee in silence. For so many weeks during the divorce proceedings she had practically hidden out in her home, not wanting to go to the grocery store or be spotted out.

She was too humiliated.

Now in a strange place she liked the fact that she could blend in, if for just a moment and enjoy a meal in silence without the looks of pity or in some cases, scorn.

"Anything else to drink with your meal, hon?" The waitress was back refilling her coffee. The name tag said Getty.

"No thank you, Getty." She smiled.

"You're new here, aren't you?" Getty smiled and fished around under the counter.

"Yes, I am." She self-consciously patted down her now-dry hair.

"Well, welcome to town. We don't have many things going on in the fall and winter months but if there is an occasional event or outing, you can find it right here in our local paper." She slid the newspaper across to her.

"Thank you."

"What's your name, hon?"

"Carolina Johnson."

"Nice to meet you Carolina. Since you're new, I'm going to give you a complimentary piece of our famous apple pie as a welcome." She lifted the lid off the pie and served her up a slice on the plate. "I always believe in eating dessert first. No point in missing out on the best things in life." She eased over to another customer and refilled his cup as she chatted him up.

Missing out on life.

Had she done that?

She'd been a housewife so long that she wasn't sure what else in life there was for her to do.

Sadness washed over her as she dug her fork into the pie.

She rarely ate dessert.

Chris had told her she was gaining weight and she'd tried everything she could to take it off.

Now over the course of weeks, she hadn't given much thought to food. Nor had she been hungry.

Even now, despite what her stomach was telling her, she wasn't hungry.

She lifted the bite of apple pie to her mouth and unfolded the paper.

By the time she was finished with her pie Getty was putting her plate in front of her.

"I see you finished your dessert. What did you think?"

"It was really good. Thank you." She blinked back tears. The waitress had done the first kind thing for her since she'd found out about Chris's affair.

"You okay, honey?" The waitress leaned forward on her elbows.

"I'm fine. Just going through some life changes." She dabbed the corners of her eyes with the paper napkin.

"Well, eat up. You can't solve your problems on an empty stomach." Getty patted her hand before turning back to the kitchen to retrieve more orders.

Carolina had a different life now, whether she liked it or not. She couldn't keep crying at the drop of a hat and feeling sorry for herself.

All she had to do was get through the day. Then she could focus on tomorrow.

She flipped through the paper as she ate her breakfast.

When she was done she waved Getty over.

"Oh, honey. You didn't eat everything."

'I know. It was just too much. Probably should have had dessert last."

"What's the fun in that?" Getty grinned and took the twenty Carolina had dug out of her purse and went to the register. When she returned she slid the change across the counter to her.

Carolina laid down a generous tip and put the rest in her wallet. "Thank you for the pie." She stood and hooked her purse on her shoulder.

"Anytime. Come back soon!" Getty called after her.

Carolina opened the door and headed for her car.

Next stop, laundromat.

CHAPTER 8

*C*arolina dug around in her purse for some loose change. When she realized all she had were bills, she went to the counter of the laundromat.

"Excuse me. Can I get some change?"

The woman with dark black hair looked up from her romance novel. "We're out of change. I sent Marcus over to the bank. He should be back soon."

"Thanks." Carolina carried her soggy sheet filled with her clothes back to the plastic chairs. She took a seat and looked at the time on her watch.

It was only nine in the morning. The day seemed to be ticking slowly by. Her room wasn't going to be ready for several hours. After eating breakfast she was tired and desperately wanted a nap.

But she didn't have the luxury.

Twenty minutes later a young man wearing athletic clothes and headphones sauntered into the laundromat. He set a brown bag on the counter and then headed back outside without even a glance in her direction.

She stood and walked back over to the lady manning the counter.

"You have change now?"

"Sure do. How much?"

Carolina slid a ten-dollar bill toward her. The woman counted out change in quarters to her.

She ended up filling two washers with her clothes. While she waited she pulled out her phone to check her emails to see if there were any messages from her attorney.

Nothing so far.

She pulled up a book on her phone and tried to read to pass the time.

When she was younger she used to read all the time. But as the years passed, Chris seemed to require more and more of her attention.

She gave up the things she used to love, to do things to satisfy him. Nights of reading with a cup of tea turned into nights of watching crime shows and football that she really didn't like.

She even tried taking up golf which he loved to do. She wasn't that good, but she figured it was an activity they would be doing together. It didn't turn out that way. He ended up playing with his friends while she was left to sit alone in the country club restaurant.

Anger and grief welled inside of her.

How much had she done and it still had not been enough for him?

Now she was left with a house that had a severe leak and was waiting on instructions from yet another man, her attorney, to tell her what to do.

She buried her head in her hands.

Twenty minutes later the washer dinged and she loaded her wet clothes into the dryer.

Another hour passed slowly. When her clothes were finally dry, she folded each item and placed them in three neat piles.

She asked permission to borrow the rolling cart to get her clothes out to her car since she didn't have a laundry basket.

The woman hesitated but finally relented.

Maybe she could see the desperation written all over her, or maybe it was just pity for someone who clearly hadn't been prepared to visit a laundromat. Whatever it was, Carolina didn't care.

After she had put her three piles of clothes in the back of her jeep her phone rang.

She dug it out of her purse.

"Hello?"

"Carolina, it's John Rithers. I've been in contact with Chris's lawyer and he says he was told by Chris the lake house was in pristine order."

"Well Chris lied," she spat out. "So what do I do now?"

"Well, I could file for an expedited hearing but that will cost you plenty of money you don't have. Instead, I advise that we get in contact with Chris to get this straightened out without court intervention."

"So do that."

"It's not that easy," he said slowly.

Carolina frowned. "Why is that?"

"Because Chris's attorney informed me that Chris left yesterday with his new wife to go to Paris. For their honeymoon."

"What?" All the strength went out of her and she slid down the back of the jeep.

"I'm afraid so. He's not expected back for three weeks."

"Three weeks? When we were married he wouldn't take a vacation longer than four days." She pressed her hand to her chest, sure that she was about to pass out in a strange town where she didn't know a soul, other than Getty at the diner.

"I'm sorry. I really am. It looks like you'll have to either get a hotel for three weeks, which you really can't afford, or make do at the lake house until things can be straightened out."

"I see," she said, lying. She didn't see. The whole thing was so unfair to her. The uncertainty of her life from minute to minute was sure to send her into a panic attack.

"I'll stay on the attorney to get in contact with Chris sooner rather than later. In the meantime hang in there."

CHAPTER 9

*C*arolina found the super center and grabbed the things on her list. If it was going to be three weeks then she was going to have to stay in the lake house while she tried to get someone out to look at the roof.

Still full from breakfast and now running on worry, she headed back to the motel to try and check in. She was told the room was now ready. She took the room key and parked in front of the room and got out. She left her items in the car and unlocked the motel door.

She cringed when she stepped inside.

It looked like an explosion from the seventies combined with a log cabin look. Wood paneled walls, yellow chenille bedspread, and furniture that looked like it had been carved out of tree limbs. A fat TV sat on the dresser and the leather recliner in the corner had a quilt laid across it. The only thing new in the room was the carpet which looked like it had recently been replaced.

She flipped the light on the bathroom wall. The tub and the sink were a matching color of avocado green reminding her of her childhood. The bathroom was dated, like the room, but it was clean.

She went back outside to grab the items she would need including the new hair dryer.

Once she settled in, Carolina pulled out the notebook she'd purchased and wrote down things that needed to be done at the lake house.

The whole house needed a deep cleaning. But it wasn't going to matter if she didn't get that roof fixed first. She pulled up a list of local roofers in the area and started calling around and set up appointment times for each to drop by the house and give her an estimate.

Then she made a list of things that she needed for the house. The first thing she added was a new mattress and bed rails for her bedroom. She could do without a chest of drawers for now, but if she was going to be able to function like a normal person, she needed a mattress.

She added new sheets and coverlet to her list. She kept jotting things down as they came to her mind. The list was growing long...and expensive.

By the time she was done it was dark outside.

She stood, stretched, and wandered over to the window, then pulled back the heavy drapery and looked out. The town's streetlights were coming on, illuminating the town in a charming way.

A minivan pulled into the parking spot next to her jeep. Two small children and their parents climbed out and pulled out suitcases. They headed to the room next door.

The squeals of children laughing struck her in the heart.

Chris had never wanted kids. Even early in their marriage when she brought up the subject, he shot her down. He said he loved it just being the two of them and didn't want a baby.

Yet here he was married to a woman half his age and expecting a child.

How much had she given up for him and been left with so little?

She swallowed down the bitterness and closed the curtain. She debated going out for dinner but she didn't feel like it. Instead she got her purse and headed for the vending machines she'd seen in the office.

When Carolina opened the door, the owner glanced up but said nothing. She went over to the machine and pulled out her leftover change from the laundromat. She put in her money and watched a granola bar drop from its slot. She lifted the plastic door and retrieved her purchase. Next, she moved to the pop machine and purchased a diet soda.

A woman with a crying baby walked in. She headed for the vending machine as she tried to soothe the baby.

The mother gave her an apologetic smile. "He's teething. And nights are the worst."

"It will get better," Carolina said, hoping to offer some encouragement.

"Thanks. I sure hope you're right." The harried mother got a soda and walked back to her room.

Carolina stuffed her granola bar in her purse and popped the top on her soda. She took a drink and headed back to her room.

Sitting on the bed she felt an overwhelming sense of loss.

Loss of her marriage.

Loss of her husband.

But what scared her the most was the feeling she'd lost herself.

CHAPTER 10

*T*he walls at the motel were paper thin.

The family with the two small kids had apparently stayed up all night watching movies because Carolina heard every word they said.

Despite all that she somehow managed a few hours of sleep. She woke at six a.m. and decided there was no use staying in bed. She had a full day ahead of her so she needed to get started.

She took a long hot shower and washed her hair. After she dressed in jeans and a sweater she dried her hair and applied a little mascara and lip gloss.

Carolina stared at her reflection in the mirror.

She noticed her clothes were looser and she hadn't realized how much weight she'd lost in her face. The dark circles from lack of sleep accentuated her now slender face. She tugged on the loose waistband.

Heading out to her car, she found a belt in the

pillowcase with her shoes before going back to her room.

She stood in front of the mirror and tugged the belt and hooked it on the last notch.

Carolina glanced at the time. Not yet seven.

There was time to grab some coffee in the office before heading over to the house.

She stepped outside and locked her room, shivering at the cool morning air. She remembered seeing a blue jean jacket in one of her piles of clothes so she retrieved it from the jeep.

Slipping it on, she huddled into her jacket as she walked to the office.

Carolina opened the door and the welcoming scent of coffee greeted her like an old friend.

"Good morning." The owner said.

"Good morning. I came to get some coffee," she smiled.

"Just finished brewing. Help yourself." He nodded toward the coffeepot. "Also have some hot oatmeal."

"Thanks." She went to the coffeepot and grabbed a mug. She poured herself a cup and grabbed some packets of sugar and creamer.

She sat down at one of the small tables and went through her email.

A message from her attorney popped up.

"Chris is definitely avoiding his attorney and any attempt to contact him. His attorney seems to be as put out as me. For right now it's estimated to be three weeks until he's back in the country. I'll keep you updated."

The coffee turned bitter in her mouth. She was on her own now. No knight in shining armor was going to show up with a new roof for her house.

She reached in her purse for her notebook. Her hand landed on her Bible. She pulled it out and looked at the first page.

Her mother had scribbled her favorite Bible verse.

"Do not be anxious about anything, but in every situation, by prayer and petition with thanksgiving, present your requests to God." ~Phillipians 4:6

"I could use a little help right now, God," she muttered to herself.

"Excuse me?" The owner looked up from reading the paper.

Carolina felt her face heat. "I was just wondering over my options for a roofer who could get to my lake house."

"Oh you have a house here?"

"Yes. It's been rented out for a while and needs some work. I have a leak. I don't know if it can be patched or needs a whole new roof. My husband…my ex-husband took care of things like that so this is all new to me." She pulled out her notebook and glanced over the list of names, embarrassed that she had told him so much.

The man walked around the desk and refilled his cup. He glanced over her shoulder and pointed at her list. "Don't use him. He's way overpriced and does shoddy work."

She looked up at him and smiled. "Thanks." Taking a pen out of her purse she crossed the name off.

The man pointed to another name. "He's good but he's backed up for weeks. Sounds like you need someone sooner rather than later."

She nodded and crossed him off as well. "Thank you. That leaves two options."

She watched his brows furrow. "I have to be honest with you. Thomas isn't the friendliest person you'll meet."

"Oh yeah?" She paused, hoping for more explanation.

"But he is honest and a hard worker," he added.

"Thank you for your honesty." She closed her notebook. "I have to cancel some meetings with some roofers." She looked his way again, and smiled. "Again, thank you. I really appreciate the input."

"Anytime." He tipped his coffee cup to her.

"And I don't think I'll be needing the room for tonight." She bit her lip.

He let out a laugh. "I was afraid of that. The walls are pretty thin. I won't charge you for last night."

"Thank you. For everything." She stood and stuffed her notebook back into her purse.

Armed with a little bit of knowledge, and a hope and a prayer, she headed to her room to pack up.

CHAPTER 11

"*M*rs. Johnson, I'm afraid you need a new roof. I could do a patch job but it would only last you a few months. The leak has gotten so bad that it's spread. And you don't want to let it go on so long that you do damage to the inside of your house." Randy Winkle shoved his hands in his jeans.

"How much is that going to cost?" She bit her lip and braced herself for the bad news.

"I came up with an estimate and wrote it down." He handed her a sheet with the estimate.

She took it, glanced down and immediately felt the air leave her lungs.

Seventeen thousand dollars!

She didn't have that kind of money on hand. This repair was going to require a bank loan, if they would even lend her that amount.

"Thank you so much for getting with me. I have one

more person giving me an estimate and then I'll let you know."

"Of course. And I do have time in my schedule. I know you want to get it done as soon as possible. I went ahead and put a tarp over the leak." He gave her a friendly smile.

"Yes I do," she assured him, trying to hide the fact the cost estimate had knocked the wind out of her. "Again, thank you for coming out. What do I owe you for the tarp?" She smiled.

He waved off her offer. "No charge."

Carolina watched him get back into his new pickup truck and slowly pull away.

She glanced at the time on her phone. She had about an hour before the other guy showed up to give her an estimate.

It was enough time to start on the kitchen and clean it up.

She walked back inside and took off her denim jacket. She shoved up her sleeves and put on her rubber gloves and started scrubbing down the kitchen counters and sink.

Once she was finished with that, she started on the oven and microwave. She scrubbed until they both shined.

Opening the cabinets, she pulled out the paper plates, her broken coffee mug, and the few cheap pots. She wiped them down and began the process of putting new shelf liner in each cupboard. She'd found some pretty pink and gray shelf paper for half-off and knew they would work well with the white cabinets.

"Hello?"

She jerked up and hit her head on a cabinet door. Grimacing she rubbed her head.

"Sorry I startled you. But I did knock." A man stared at her from the living room. He had jet black hair and deep blue eyes that were glaring at her with impatience. He wore jeans and a black long-sleeve T-shirt. He held a pair of leather gloves in his right hand which, judging by the callouses, had seen a lot of manual labor.

She scowled at him. "Do you always enter people's homes without an invitation?"

"Yes. Especially when I've been invited to come over for an estimate." He cocked his head, daring her to challenge him further.

She tugged off her rubber gloves. "I need a new roof."

"I know. That's why I'm here." He acted like he was bored and had better things to do.

"Mr. …."

"My name is Thomas Harding."

"Mr. Harding." She nodded. "I'm Carolina Johnson. The owner of the house."

He looked around. "Where's your husband?"

She lifted her chin. "I'm divorced. I am the owner of the house."

With arms crossed over his chest he furrowed his brows.

"My roof has a leak," she continued. "I need an estimate. I've already had one man give me an estimate."

"I bet it was Randy Winkle."

"How did you know?"

"Because he seems to think he is my competition." He slapped his gloves on his thigh and walked over to the large picture window. He stared out at the lake.

"Is he your competition?" She narrowed her eyes not sure if she should trust someone who just barges in someone's house.

"He's more likeable than me so he gets more business. If you want someone to hold your hand and coddle you throughout the process, then I am not that man."

Anger flared in her veins. "And what are you the man for?"

"Honestly? I do better work. And I can fix your roof at a better price."

"Do you have an estimate for me?" She gripped the back of the couch and watched him. She felt like she needed some distance from this tornado of a man.

He pulled out a notepad from his back pocket. He wrote something down and pulled off the paper and handed it to her.

She held his gaze and took the paper. She glanced down and frowned. "This is cheaper than the other estimate."

"That's because I don't have a lot of overhead. I work alone, except for getting the old roof off, so I don't have to pay other workers. I arrive early and work until late. If you are a late sleeper then you're not going to want to hire me," he warned.

"I am an early riser." She narrowed her eyes. "Mr. Harding, ..."

"Call me Thomas."

"Thomas." She sighed. "You don't really act like you want this job. Can you tell me why?"

He shrugged. "I prefer to deal with men. I don't have time for idle chatter or friendship. I prefer to be left alone when I work."

"I see."

"Do you?" He seemed to be studying her.

"Well Mr. Harding. I'll let you know in a few days if you have the job." She lifted her chin and showed him to the door.

As soon as she closed the front door she ran to the window and peered out.

Thomas Harding drove an older model Ford F250. It wasn't new and shiny with all the bells and whistles like Randy Winkle's truck.

Thomas Harding was the kind of man who was brutally honest, even when his comments would chafe. The guy seemed confident he could do the job, and at a much lower price. Yet, given his demeanor could she hire someone like that?

With time ticking away, she was going to have to make a decision soon.

CHAPTER 12

*A*fter Thomas left, Carolina spent the rest of the day scrubbing the house. When she finished, the kitchen sparkled and the living room was dust free. She had even managed to get the stains out of the couch with the cleaner she picked up at the store.

She also cleaned the living room and put the area rug on the back deck where she beat it to get the rest of the dust out that the vacuum left behind.

What little furniture that was left in the living room, made it easy to get the wood floor cleaned. She inspected the floor by the foyer where it had leaked. From the looks of things she could probably get away with just replacing the boards that had gotten wet.

Carolina went to the shed in the backyard and found a box of wood flooring that matched. She would get on the internet tonight and find a tutorial about how to replace a few boards of flooring before she attempted it. At some point she knew she was going to have to refinish the flooring.

But that would have to wait. She simply didn't have the funds.

Next she moved into the master bathroom to give it a good cleaning. Admittedly she liked cleaning. When she was cleaning she didn't have time to worry about her leaky roof, or her broken heart.

Her mother always said that a well-kept and tidy home could heal the soul.

The first time she'd said that their family had just moved into her grandmother's house to help care for her.

The house was old and in need of repair. Despite her young age, she managed to help her father while he made repairs to the place. She handed him the screwdriver to install a new window, or opened a can of paint for the walls, or helped plant seeds in the abandoned garden in the backyard.

The house seemed to come to life with each stroke of a paintbrush or scrub of a window.

Each completed task brought renewal, both for the house and for her spirit. It felt good to see something so in need of repair get restored.

Maybe she could use this lake house to help heal a part of her that had been destroyed.

Carolina sat on the floor and leaned back against the wall of the bathroom. She still needed to bring in the new towels and washcloths she bought along with the other items for the bathroom.

She sighed and scrambled off the floor.

She needed to call and find out who could come and get the mattress and take it to the dump. Then she would have to get a new mattress to sleep on. She'd gotten so busy and let time slip away that now it was too late to try to find a furniture store.

She shook her head and walked into the kitchen and pulled out a bottle of water from the refrigerator. She took a long drink and looked around at her progress.

Still so much to do. She wasn't sure how much money she had either. She needed to check her account before she bought anything else.

She sighed and looked out at the lake.

She saw a flash of movement on her deck. She froze.

The nearest house was not that close and she was not expecting anyone this late. It was almost nine o'clock.

With her heart thumping in her chest she pulled open the drawer. Her hand landed on a plastic knife.

She groaned in frustration. She should have bought some proper silverware when she was shopping but hadn't put it on the list.

She certainly couldn't defend herself with a piece of plastic.

Gathering up every bit of courage, she edged closer to the back door that led out onto the deck.

The dark figure was crouched near the patio furniture. With a trembling hand she flipped the light switch.

She squinted.

The figure darted from under the chair to the end of the steps on four legs.

It was a black dog.

Filled with relief she opened the door and stepped outside. "What are you doing here? Are you lost?" She edged closer.

She noticed the skeletal frame of the black dog and realized the poor animal had not eaten in a while. She wrapped her arms around herelf as the wind picked up.

"I've got some food for you little guy." She walked back inside but didn't close the door. She didn't want to scare him off.

She pulled out a paper plate and made a sandwich. She cut the food into tiny pieces and then grabbed a plastic bowl from underneath the sink and ran some water in it. She turned and then stopped.

The black dog had come inside and curled up on one of her bags with the towels in it.

"Hey, you can't sleep there. I need those towels." She scowled but didn't have the heart to make him move.

"Fine. At least come eat." She set the plate of food and water down near the dog.

He eyed her and slowly stood and sniffed the food before scarfing it down.

She walked over to the door and shut it. The dog was now standing and looking at her as if he didn't agree with her shutting the door.

"Look it's too cold to leave the door open. Besides it's not safe." She shrugged and walked into the kitchen. Her stomach rumbled, signaling she'd not eaten all day.

She made herself a sandwich and added some chips to the plate. Grabbing a bottle of water she sat down on the couch.

The black dog had finished its food and walked over to her and sat at her feet.

"I've already fed you. Now you sit there and be good. Any nonsense out of you and you will go back outside."

Carolina took a bite of her sandwich while the dog watched her closely, eyeing her sandwich.

She made it halfway through her meal when she shook her head. "Fine. Take the rest." She held out the half-eaten sandwich.

The dog gently took it out of her hand.

After he finished off the sandwich, he slowly edged toward her and sniffed her fingers.

"See I'm not going to hurt you," she said softly.

The dog seemed to understand her words and tucked his head close to her leg.

She slowly reached down and rubbed his head. When she stopped he put his paw up on her arm.

"More huh?" She laughed and gently petted him.

She stood up and looked at him. "You have to belong to someone around here." She looked but he didn't have a collar. "Has someone abandoned you?" She shook her head in sympathy. "I know the feeling."

The dog's ears perked up.

"I'm going to take a bath and go to bed. So stay right there until I get my towels out of the bag."

She pulled her new towels out of the bag and headed into the bathroom. She hadn't thought about picking up any bubble bath or bath salts when she was shopping. It didn't matter. She would be more than satisfied relaxing in a hot bath of any kind after all the work she'd done on the house. She ran the water in the tub and waited for it to fill.

She grabbed her pajamas from the pile of freshly laundered clothes and laid them on the counter. Slipping off her clothes she sunk into the hot water and closed her eyes.

Her body ached. But it was her heart that hurt more.

Chris and Kylie were in Paris having a luxurious time while she was at her leaky lake house with no bed to sleep in and a stray dog.

"Figures." She muttered to herself. Somehow she always thought in the back of her mind that she didn't deserve the life she was living.

She suspected it wouldn't last.

She had been right.

She felt something cold on her hand. She opened her eyes to find the dog resting his cold nose on her hand in a gesture of compassion.

"Thanks boy." She patted his head. "You want a bath too? It would make you feel better. Looks like you haven't had a bath in a long time."

The dog sat obediently as she got out of the tub.

She toweled off and slipped on her pajamas.

She bent to let the water out, but the dog jumped in before she could pull the plug.

Sitting in the water he looked at her, waiting for her to bathe him.

She laughed. "I was going to use the shower head but apparently you prefer baths."

She grabbed an older towel from under the cabinet and put it down on the floor by the tub.

She knelt and slowly cupped water in her hands to get the dog wet. She took the shampoo and poured out a liberal amount and began massaging the liquid into his fur.

He stared up at her as she worked.

"It's okay boy. I promise this will make you feel like a million bucks."

When it came time to rinse him, she had to cup her hands to pour water down his back. She was going to have to be more prepared next time and keep a plastic cup in the bathroom for such things.

She stopped. "Maybe there won't be another time. Maybe your owners lost you and they'll be coming for you soon." While she would be happy for him to return to his family, the idea brought a little touch of sadness.

When she was finished washing him off she pulled the plug on the tub.

She reached for the towel just as the dog jumped out of the tub. He shook, sending water droplets everywhere.

She squealed and held up the towel in front of her.

She scowled at the dog. "Give me a warning next time."

He blinked at her and then yawned. She towel dried the dog as best as she could.

"Let's find you someplace to sleep." She turned the lights off in the bathroom and headed into the living room.

The dog put its paw on the couch and looked at her with big brown eyes.

"Sorry buddy. That's where I'm sleeping. You have to sleep over there," she pointed. " I'll make you a comfortable bed."

She went into the laundry room and found an old but clean blanket. She folded it into a large square and placed it in front of the fireplace.

It would be getting cold soon and it would be nice to have a fire. She wasn't sure if the fireplace was in good working order or not. Maybe whoever she hired to fix the roof would know something about fireplaces.

She dug around in the plastic shopping bags and pulled out the new sheets she'd bought. She fixed up the couch as a bed. Until she got a mattress she was going to have to couch surf.

She fluffed up her pillow and put the coverlet she found at the discount store on top of the sheet. She sat on the couch until the dog went over and curled up on his make-shift bed.

"Good dog,"

Carolina laid down and pulled the coverlet over her. Her fingers traced the intricate outline of the stitching. It made her think of her mother and how she loved to sew. Most of all she loved to quilt. Her mother always gave her quilts away as gifts. The last quilt her mother made had been gifted to her. She always had the quilt draped over her favorite chair in her bedroom. In the winter months she would curl up with a cup of coffee and spread her quilt over her legs and sit in the silence of the morning.

The quilt pattern was Hanging Gardens and it was done in an array of greens and golds. It truly was stunning and everyone always commented on it when they saw it.

She loved that quilt.

But Kylie had thrown it away like garbage.

Grief washed over her like a tsunami and she was reminded of how truly alone she was.

Hot tears trailed down her cheeks onto her pillow. Her quiet weeping turned into hard sobs.

The last thing that she thought of as she cried herself to sleep was why this happening to her.

CHAPTER 13

*C*arolina woke the next morning and turned over, wanting a few extra minutes before she climbed out from the warmth of the blanket. As she did she felt a strange weight on her legs. Sitting up on the couch, she saw that during the night the dog had climbed onto the couch with her.

She tried moving her legs but they had fallen asleep.

"Come on boy. You need to move." She nudged the dog with her hand.

He lifted his head, yawned and slowly climbed off the couch.

Carolina swung her legs off the side of the couch and rubbed the feeling back into her legs.

She headed into the kitchen and pulled the coffee from the cabinet. She made quick work of getting the coffee started. She glanced up and saw the dog standing by the back door.

"I'm coming." She grabbed the coverlet and

wrapped it around herself before opening the back door and facing the chilly air.

The dog bolted out onto the deck and down the steps into the backyard, where he promptly relieved himself by the large oak tree.

She followed him out onto the deck and looked at the sun rising over the lake.

The wind was cool but it looked like it was going to be a beautiful day.

She stayed outside long enough for the coffee to finish brewing and then whistled for the dog.

The dog looked up from sniffing something in a clump of dead grass.

"Are you coming inside or not?"

The dog lowered his head.

"Suit yourself."

She turned and headed straight for the kitchen to fix her coffee. After grabbing her broken mug she sat down on the couch and reached for her phone. She pulled up the weather forecast.

It was clear for the next few days but next week's forecast included a forty-percent chance of rain.

She had to make a decision about a roofer... and soon. But before that, she needed to figure out how she was going to pay for it.

She checked her email for a message from her attorney.

Nothing.

Worry settled in the pit of her stomach. It was early

but she had to get some answers one way or another. She needed to make a decision quick.

She fired off a quick text to her attorney regarding the desperate need for a roof and the impending bad weather.

After sending the message she put the phone on the coffee table, curled her legs underneath her, and sipped on her coffee.

Carolina supposed she could see if the bank would lend her money to repair the roof. With the amount of her alimony payments, and the little bit of savings, she could pay the loan back over time.

Even without a job, she had enough to live on for a few months, maybe more if she budgeted well.

Getting off the couch she went to the foyer where the leak had sprung. It was no longer leaking but there was a large dark stain on the ceiling.

She had two options for roofers. While the first guy was more agreeable and had gone out of his way to cover her roof with a tarp, her mind kept drifting back to Thomas.

From the look of his clothes, to the calloused hands, he appeared to be a hard worker.

Then again, looks could be deceiving. Her ex-husband appeared to be a nice guy and look what happened.

Carolina sighed heavily. First things first. She had to go to the bank.

Finishing her coffee, she washed and dried her

coffee cup. Carolina went to the back door to let the dog back in but he was nowhere in sight.

She was disappointed but didn't have time to dwell on it. He probably went back to his owner. Convinced the dog was back at home, she headed back to the bathroom to get dressed for the day.

CHAPTER 14

*C*arolina had chosen a pair of tan slacks and a black button-up shirt from her closet. The weather was nice and she didn't feel the need for a jacket so instead she had opted for a simple gold necklace and bracelet. It was the only jewelry she had left since it was what she'd worn on the last day she left her house.

As she walked to the front door of the bank she took a few deep cleansing breaths to calm her nerves.

Opening the door, she saw that the small lobby was practically empty.

A woman at one of the desks made eye contact and smiled. "May I help you with something?"

"Yes." She smiled and walked over. "I would like to talk to someone about a home-improvement loan."

"I can help with that. Please have a seat." She pointed to the chair on the other side of her desk. "My name is Rebecca Sims. I'm the loan officer." They shook hands.

"I'm Carolina Johnson. Nice to meet you." She sat down in the leather chair.

"Are you new here?"

"I am. I own a lake house and I need a new roof. I was hoping to get a bank loan for that."

"Oh, which lake house do you own?" Rebecca leaned forward. "My grandmother lives on the lake."

"It's 4500 Laurel Cove. The red house with the deck."

Rebecca's smile slid off her face. "I know the house."

Carolina's gut twisted.

"So you're living in it now?" Rebecca cocked her head.

"Yes. I...I recently got the house in my divorce settlement." She twisted the wedding band on her finger.

"My grandmother told me it had renters who caused a lot of trouble on the lake." Rebecca frowned. Gone was the friendly welcoming vibe she'd picked up earlier.

"That's what I heard as well. I'm terribly sorry for that. My husband took care of renting it out. I had no idea there had been issues." She glanced down at her hands clasped in her lap. "Or the fact it had not been taken care of. I'm trying to remedy that now."

"I see." Rebecca punched some keys into her computer. "Do you have the documentation proving you own the house? Perhaps a quitclaim deed?" She looked up at her.

"I do."Carolina reached inside her purse and dug out the folded papers and slid them across the desk to her.

Rebecca studied the paperwork and typed something else into the computer.

She tried to read her expression but Rebecca had quite the poker face.

"Do you mind if I ask you a personal question? Just curious, how long were you married?"

Carolina cleared her throat. "Twenty years."

"That long?" She arched an eyebrow. "I'm sorry it didn't end well. I was married ten."

Carolina shook her head. "I'm sorry."

Rebecca waved her off. "Don't be. Sadly some things aren't meant to last."

"I thought marriage was supposed to last until 'death do you part'. At least that's what we both said in our vows." Carolina wasn't sure why she kept telling this woman about her personal life. But she couldn't seem to shut up.

"So he left you?" Rebecca frowned and cocked her head.

"Yes. For a woman half his age." Carolina bit her lip.

Rebecca didn't seem surprised. She straightened her shoulders and looked across the desk. "My husband left me for my sister. I haven't seen either of them since they left and took all my savings. That was five years ago."

"That's awful. I'm sorry." Carolina couldn't imagine. The woman's story was worse than hers.

Rebecca shrugged. "Don't be. It took time but I moved on. His loss."

Carolina's heart tugged for the woman. "I found out at a party where all our friends were." She blinked. "Now looking back on it, they all knew. But didn't tell me."

"Then they don't sound like very good friends."

Carolina nodded. "You're right. I need to be more selective. In friends as well as husbands."

"Your husband will regret leaving you. They usually do. Or so my therapist said." She shook her head.

"I doubt that. He got her pregnant."

Rebecca's eyes widened.

"And they are currently on a honeymoon in Paris, where I cannot get in touch with him about the repairs needed on this house." Her words held a spark of anger.

Rebecca stopped typing and looked at her. "He married her?"

"Yes. So you see, he won't regret it."

"How old is the guy?"

"We are both forty."

"Does he realize he's going to be attending the kid's high school graduation when he's almost sixty?" Rebecca snorted.

Carolina shrugged slightly. "I guess so."

"He'll be paying for at least four years of college after that." Rebecca snorted again. "I'll stand by my statement. He'll regret what he did. Eventually. It's all fun and games until the young wife wants to go club-bing and all he wants is to watch Netflix and grill."

That brought a smile to Carolina's face. "I didn't think about it that way."

"You should." Rebecca lifted her chin. "Again, it's their loss, not ours."

"Thank you. Regardless of what happens with the loan, I appreciate your encouraging words." Carolina felt lighter.

Rebecca went back to her typing. "So do you have a job yet?"

"No, but I have alimony. For a while." She bit her lip. "I know I should be looking but I don't know what I would be good at. I never went to college. Just married Chris right out of high school."

Rebecca nodded. "In order to get a home equity line-of-credit we are going to need to see paperwork proving expected alimony. The suits upstairs are kind of wiggy about extending credit when they can't assure the income is there to pay the loan back. You understand?"

Carolina thought that made sense. In fact, none of what Rebecca said came as a surprise. She nodded. "Okay, sure. I can try and get you whatever you need."

"In addition, we will need an estimate of how much the roof repairs are going to cost."

"Oh, I have that already. I had two different guys come out and give me an estimate." She pulled those papers out of her purse and handed them to Rebecca.

Rebecca nodded at the first estimate and then

looked at the scrap of paper. A small grin crossed her lips. "You called Thomas Harding."

"Yes. Do you know him?"

She grinned and nodded. "Have you decided on who to use?"

"Well, Randy was very polite and even covered the leak with a tarp at no charge to me. Thomas seemed knowledgeable, but he wasn't all that personable, if you want to know the truth. In fact, he edged on being a little rude."

"But you didn't rule him out?"

"Well, no. He gave me the impression he would be a hard worker. And I'm trying to learn to not make decisions based on emotions."

Rebecca smiled and handed her Thomas's estimate. "I'll give you the loan as long as you use Thomas."

"Really?" She felt her eyes light up.

"Yes. You seem trustworthy. I can write up this request and present it. But you also need to bring me in a written plan of where you are looking for employment. I don't care if it's folding laundry at the laundromat, just as long as it's employment."

"Thank you." Carolina felt relief fill her body. She stuck out her hand.

Rebecca shook her hand. "In the meantime, we'll send out an assessor to get the house valued. I am confident it will appraise high. So go ahead and hire Thomas, before the rain hits." She smiled.

"I will, and again, thank you." Carolina stood and hooked her purse on her shoulder.

She got into her car and for the first time in a while, she smiled. And she felt it all the way to her toes.

CHAPTER 15

*C*arolina called and left a message on Thomas's phone, informing him that he got the job. Afterward she treated herself to a breakfast at the diner and had a nice conversation with Getty. Getty was the one who told her to go to Second Hand Furniture to find a dryer. She said all their stuff was basically new just had some dings on it from the factory.

After breakfast she took Getty's advice and headed to Second Hand Furniture. Luckily she found a dryer that would be delivered that afternoon. She also found a new mattress and added it to the delivery as well. Now all she needed was a bed frame.

She headed back to her jeep. A store window decked out with pumpkins and leaves caught her eye.

Maggie's Treasures.

It was the antique store that the guy at the motel had mentioned.

She still needed some dishes for the kitchen. Maybe

she could find a set of used dishes for cheap. The dryer and mattress were well under budget which would give her plenty of available funds, if the prices were right.

She looked both ways before she crossed the street.

There was a pretty glass cake stand with decorative cupcakes perched on a refurbished rolling cart in the window display of the antique store. Whoever owned the shop, certainly had an eye for decorating.

She opened the door and stepped inside. The scent of floor polish and lemon cleaner hit her nostrils. Everything was so neat and orderly.

Shelves filled with everything one might need for a home lined the whole shop.

"Welcome. Can I help you look for anything?" A young woman in her thirties smiled from behind the counter. She was busy wrapping up a set of champagne glasses in protective paper.

"I need a lot actually. Dishes and maybe some silverware for my kitchen?"

The girl pointed. "You'll find those on aisle three."

"You don't happen to have bedroom furniture do you?"

"Actually, we just got a bed frame in today. I'm sorry, but there's no dresser or chest of drawers to go with it."

Carolina shrugged and smiled. "That's okay."

"The items you are looking for will be all the way in the back near aisle six. If you have any questions let me know. My name is Jennifer."

"Thanks, Jennifer."

She took her time getting to aisle three. Everything commanded her attention. She found some candlesticks that would look great on her mantle but she had to control her urge to buy them. Right now she just needed the basics.

When she stepped on aisle three she saw sets of dishes in every kind of pattern and color. She found a pink and blue chintz pattern that captured her attention right away. It was a complete place setting of twelve and included teacups and a teapot.

There was another set of dishes that was just as pretty. It was a white and blue floral pattern but it didn't have the tea cups or tea pot.

"Oh, are you interested in the Summer Chintz Pattern?" Jennifer knelt and placed a teapot on the bottom shelf.

"I am. But I'm afraid to know the price."

Jennifer laughed. She picked up a plate and looked at the bottom. "You're right. No price there." She continued to pick through the dishes checking for the price.

Jennifer finally looked up at her. "I can't find a price so why don't you make me an offer?

"Are you serious?" Carolina gaped at her.

"Sure." She laughed. "Sometimes I get items in and forget to price them. It doesn't happen very often. So this must be your lucky day."

"I haven't had a lucky day in a while." Carolina muttered.

"Then it's time you should." Jennifer stood and brushed her hands on her pants.

"I don't know what's a reasonable amount to offer. How much would you take?"

"You're not a very good negotiator." Jennifer propped her hands on her hips.

"I know." Carolina sighed. "Normally it would probably cost a few hundred dollars."

"True. But it's not new and I could use the shelf space. Dishes are something that I have too much of as it is."

"Okay. How about a hundred dollars?"

The front door dinged and Jennifer frowned. "I tell you what. I'll let you have the set for seventy-five dollars if you wrap it yourself."

Carolina felt her spirits lift. "Deal." She stuck out her hand.

They shook. "I'll bring you a box and some paper. When you're done meet me at the desk."

Jennifer brought her a large box and some newspaper.

Carolina sat on the floor cross-legged and began carefully wrapping her new dishes.

When she was finally done she brought the box to the front counter.

Jennifer was assisting another customer so she left the box on the counter and went in search of the furniture.

She looked through the antique side tables that were

marked a little too pricey for her budget. She found a large mirror that would look good in the dining room. But she reminded herself she was here for a bed frame.

She spotted the headboard resting against the wall and stepped closer.

The piece was a queen-size Victorian headboard with a matching footboard. The headboard was scalloped and had a bouquet of flowers painted in the middle.

It was old but beautiful and something about it struck a cord with Carolina.

She looked for the price tag and held it up. "Two hundred dollars. That can't be right."

Jennifer appeared at her side. "I see you found what you were looking for."

"Two hundred dollars?" She arched her brow. "That's all?"

"Yes, for the bed. It's a fair price given I actually got it for a lot less. Plus, there's no matching furniture that goes with it."

"I'll take it." Carolina frowned. "But I have no way to carry it home. I had to get the Second Hand shop to deliver my mattress and my dryer to my house this afternoon."

"Oh that's no problem. I'll call over there and have them take the bed out to you as well."

"They'll do that?"

"Of course they will. The owner is my cousin Freddy."

"Perfect. Then add that to my total."

Jennifer smiled. "Anything else today? I think you mentioned silverware?"

"Thanks for reminding me."

"Look on aisle one."

"Thanks." Carolina smiled as Jennifer went to call her cousin.

Carolina made her way over to the aisle and quickly picked out a set of silverware that was reasonably priced. It wasn't sterling and that was fine by her. As long as she didn't have to eat on plastic utensils, she'd be happy.

In fact, today had been a really good day. On the way home, she felt her hopes rising. Maybe, just maybe things were going to be okay after all.

CHAPTER 16

*C*arolina pulled into her driveway and killed the engine. The old woman who had confronted her earlier when she had been asleep in her car was pounding on the front door.

She groaned and jumped out of the car. "Can I help you?"

"Yes. You can. One of my cats was attacked this morning by a black dog. A dog which I saw running into your backyard."

"Oh no." She shook her head.

The woman put her hands on her hips. "That is the second time this has happened."

"It's not my dog. He showed up last night." She held up her hands. "I tried to see if he had a name on his collar but nothing. I figured he was a stray."

"If he was a stray, why did he return to your house?" She narrowed her eyes as if she didn't believe her.

Carolina weighed her answer. "Probably because I fed him last night. He was a skeleton when he showed up."

"Well since you've adopted him you have adopted his problems." She shoved her finger in Carolina's chest.

Carolina blinked and stepped back, shocked at the old woman's attitude toward her. "What does that mean?"

"You're paying the vet bills for my cat."

Carolina gasped. "What?"

The sound of a truck pulling up had them both turning.

Thomas Harding.

He got out of the truck and glared at both of them.

"What is he doing here?" The old woman asked.

"He's fixing my roof." Carolina reported.

Thomas walked over. "I got your message. And I also heard from Rebecca to go ahead and replace the roof. She said she already sent the assessor over here this afternoon."

"Wait. Rebecca from the bank? My Rebecca?" The old woman narrowed her eyes at her.

"Yes. I met her at the bank this morning." Carolina said carefully.

"What are you doing here, Bernice?" Thomas cocked his head and rubbed his chin.

She lifted her chin and glared. "Her dog attacked my cat and I want her to pay for the vet bill."

"Well, stand in line. She's paying for a roof first." He walked past her to the side of the house and looked up.

Carolina blinked, not sure if Thomas just insulted her or defended her.

The old woman snarled and stormed away down the driveway.

Stunned Carolina walked over to Thomas. "Who is she? That's the second time she's appeared and accused me of something."

"That's Bernice. She lives in the lake house a few houses down from you. She's lived out here as long as I can remember."

Carolina turned and watched the woman pump her arms as she stormed away.

"For someone so old she sure has a lot of spunk."

"That's not spunk. That's just pure meanness. Don't ever make her mad."

"Too late. She said my last renters were loud and threw parties. And claimed one of them ran into the neighbor's mailbox."

He frowned. "Probably Hannah's."

Feeling a headache coming on she rubbed her temple. "And now she claims that my dog attacked her cat."

"I didn't see a dog when I was over here yesterday."

"That's because I don't have a dog. One showed up last night and I fed it. I guess she saw it run over here and thinks it's mine. You wouldn't know if anyone is missing a black dog would you?"

"No." He answered quickly.

He wasn't much for small talk.

She cocked her head. "So what is your expected time of completing this contract? I saw on the weather forecast that it's predicted to rain next week."

"I'll get it done before then." He walked around the house and studied the roof.

She wrapped her arms around herself and unease welled up inside her. Maybe she should have hired the other guy.

But it was too late now.

"I guess you'll start tomorrow?" she prompted.

His brows furrowed and he turned to face her. "Tomorrow? No. I'm starting today."

"Today? Are you prepared for that?"

"I've brought my supplies. I've ordered the shingles already. They will be here tomorrow."

She nodded with relief, glad he didn't plan on delaying the project. She was anxious for the project to be completed, even though she couldn't seem to squelch her nerves over such a large amount of money she was about to go into debt over.

She followed him to his truck. "You seem very prepared."

"I don't like to waste time." He turned back to his truck and stopped. "And don't let your dog around my ladder. I don't have any desire to fall and break my back."

As if on cue, the black dog darted out from the backyard and stopped. He seemed to be sizing Thomas up.

Carolina let out a heavy sigh. "He's not my dog."

The dog walked over and sat by her feet. He nudged her hand with his head.

Thomas snorted. "Then you should tell him that. I don't think he knows."

CHAPTER 17

*C*arolina left Thomas to his work as she turned her attention to unpacking her car. She unloaded boxes of her new dishes and silverware and carried them inside the house which required several trips. When she'd finished unloading, she unpacked and put her housewares away. She was nearly finished when there was a knock at the door.

She shut the kitchen drawer and went to the front door. She glanced around for the dog, but he was nowhere to be found.

She opened the door.

"Hello ma'am. I have your delivery." A young man in jeans and a black T-shirt glanced down at his clip-board. Sitting in the driveway was a large unmarked moving truck.

"Hello." She looked over his shoulder. "I didn't expect you to arrive so soon. I thought it would be after twelve."

"Our other delivery went faster than we thought. Jennifer told me you're new here. Figured you'd want the bed and dryer set up the sooner the better."

"Thanks. I appreciate it." She glanced at the door. "Do you think the door is wide enough to fit everything through?"

He examined the door jamb. "I think it will fit. Want to show me the room where these things will be going?"

"Sure, come on in." She waved him inside. "I just got here a few days ago. Trying to get things settled as I go."

"I've never actually been inside this house. I'm Lance Matthews by the way." He held out his hand.

"Carolina Johnson." She shook his hand. "Do you deliver out here a lot?"

"Oh, yes. The owner four houses down is remodeling her whole house. She's been keeping us busy. Mrs. Wilford. Have you met her?"

"No, not yet. Bernice is the only person I've met in the neighborhood and I'm pretty sure she doesn't like me."

He laughed. "She doesn't like anyone. Except Rebecca. Her granddaughter."

That pulled a laugh out of Carolina.

She turned the light on in the laundry room. "This is where I need the dryer. I've swept and cleaned in here but I'm not sure how to hook it up."

"I can do that for you. I've hooked up just about every appliance there is."

"That would be wonderful. Thank you so much. And down this hall is the bedroom." She flipped the light switch. Her gaze landed on the old mattress.

"I don't suppose you would take this old mattress with you if I paid you a little extra?"

"I can do that. I'll be going by the dump on my next delivery."

"Perfect. Do you need me for anything else?"

"No ma'am. We will get everything in and hooked up."

"I'll get out of your way then." She watched as he returned to his truck. She found a towel and wedged it under the door to keep it open.

She went back to the kitchen to pull something out of the freezer for dinner.

She had grown tired of sandwiches and snacks. She longed for a hot meal. Something she hadn't had in weeks.

She pulled out the small pot roast, put it in the sink, and ran some water.

As she worked the men carried her dryer into the laundry room.

Suddenly the black dog appeared at her side and sat beside her.

She frowned. "How'd you get in here?"

He cocked his head.

"You know you are getting me in trouble with the neighbors. You shouldn't have attacked that cat. Now I've got to pay another bill I can't afford."

Again, the dog just looked at her like he understood what she was saying.

"We've got your dryer hooked up and the old mattress moved out. Do you want the bed set up in the same place?" Freddy asked her.

"Can you put the bed facing the large window?"

"Sure can." He smiled.

She dried her hands on the towel, headed into the bedroom, and went to work.

She grabbed a broom and gave the floors a good cleaning, catching any dust bunnies that had escaped the first round of sweeping.

She stood where the headboard would go and looked out the large sliding glass window. This would be a better fit, having the sunrise over the lake to wake her up. She still needed a night stand but that could come later when she could afford it. Right now, she just needed the basics.

"Here we go," Freddy announced as he carried in the headboard and his buddy carried in the footboard.

After retrieving the bedrails they quickly assembled the bed. "Do you want us to move this closer to the wall?"

"No. I think I'll keep it like this until I have time to paint the walls."

"Then we'll bring in your new mattress." He headed out of the room.

She went and retrieved the sheets she slept on the night before.

The two men came back into the bedroom and cut

away the plastic from the mattress. The new mattress was then placed on the bed. The two guys stepped back and looked at her.

"What do you think?" Freddy asked.

"I think I'll have a real bed to sleep on instead of the couch. My back thanks you."

They laughed.

"Can I get you two anything to drink? I've got some bottled water."

"That would be nice, actually."

She hurried into the kitchen and pulled out two bottles. She opened the cupboard and found a couple of granola bars. She brought them to the men. "I hope you like granola bars. I haven't had time to bake since I got here."

"That's awfully nice of you." Freddy took the offered snacks. "Thank you. Is there anything else I can do for you?"

"I think that's it. How much do I owe for delivery?"

He shook his head and took a drink of the water. "Nothing. I was headed out this way anyway."

She frowned. "Are you sure?"

"I'm sure. But we do have to get going. Nice meeting you." He gave a wave as they walked up the walkway toward the delivery truck.

She waved and then shut the door before heading into the bedroom. She could hear Thomas walking around on the roof and wondered if he was okay by himself.

She made up the bed and put the new coverlet on

top. Stepping back she looked at the progress. The bed looked great but it accentuated how badly she needed to paint the yellowed walls.

As she set the room to rights, she heard some loud voices outside. She walked out the back and saw Thomas and an older man standing in the backyard talking loudly.

She folded her arms across her chest. "What's going on?"

"This is Stanley." Thomas said in a loud voice. "He's going to help me take the old roof off."

Stanley was busy looking out over the lake. Thomas elbowed him in the stomach to get his attention.. The older man gruffed and turned around. He seemed surprised to see her standing there.

A smile slowly grew as he tipped his cowboy hat to her.

"Hello." She smiled politely."Can I get you two some water?"

Stanley just stood there and smiled. Puzzled, she looked over at Thomas.

Thomas shook his head and leaned closer to Stanley. "She wants to know if you want something to drink." He yelled in the man's face.

Startled, Carolina took a step back. Stanley was old enough to be Thomas's father. He should have more respect for his elders.

Stanley didn't seem to mind. He nodded slowly and turned to her. "I'd like a beer."

Thomas glared. "He will not have a beer. Water is fine."

She laughed nervously. "Good because water is all I have." She went back inside. When she came back outside Thomas was yelling at Stanley again. The older man ducked his head.

She walked over to him and thrust the waters at Thomas. "Can I have a word with you?"

"Make it quick." He handed one of the waters to Stanley and walked over to the large oak tree near the water.

"Mr. Harding, I don't know what kind of relationship you have with Stanley," she glanced over her shoulder and then back at him, "and I know he is your employee. But I have to say, that I don't like the way you were talking to him. Yelling at him like that. He's an old man. And he deserves respect." She crossed her arms over her chest.

Treating someone badly didn't sit well with her.

Maybe because she'd been disrespected by her ex.

Maybe it was because Thomas didn't seem to care about other people's feelings.

Whatever it was, it had her emotions snowballing until she couldn't hold back her feelings any more.

Thomas looked at her and blinked with confusion. Then his face split into a grin.

She was shocked to see the man was actually handsome when he wasn't scowling.

"Mrs. Johnson…"

"Carolina." She lifted her chin.

"Carolina. I wasn't yelling at Stanley because you think I'm some horrible person. I was yelling at him because I have to. He can't hear a thing. He's almost deaf."

She dropped her arms, caught off guard by this new information. "Oh, I see. Well, maybe he needs to have hearing aids then."

"Won't do any good. I bought him hearing aids three months ago. He refuses to wear them."

She frowned. "Why is that?"

"He says he doesn't need them." He leaned forward. "And just to let you know, if you have any alcohol in the house you might want to lock it up. He's also a recovering alcoholic who falls off the wagon on a frequent basis. We all watch out for him and work to keep him sober. Keeps our hands full because Stanley has a lot of crafty ways to maneuver a drink. Might say, it's his favorite pastime."

"Oh. I had no idea." Her eyes darted back to the old man who was now patting the black dog who had reappeared.

"Don't worry. He's not going to steal anything. And if he does manage to dig up a bottle, the worst he'll do is strip off his clothes and go jump in the lake."

"But it's cold."

Thomas shrugged. "When he gets drunk, he doesn't feel a thing."

What had she gotten herself into?

Thomas slapped his work gloves against his pants. "Is there anything else or can we get back to work?"

"That's all." She said sheepishly. She watched as Thomas and Stanley returned to the task of unloading the back of his truck.

She headed inside to mind her own business.

CHAPTER 18

*C*arolina grabbed a cup of coffee and walked out onto her deck. The sunrise was beautiful as it rose over the lake. The air was chilly and she wrapped the throw she'd bought across her shoulders and settled into a chair. The black dog found his way out into the yard and was nose-down in the grass, exploring all the different smells.

Carolina contemplated the fact she had bills coming in and she would soon have to find employment. It was unlikely her alimony payments would cover every-thing. She would also have to go into town to sign the paperwork for the loan. Rebecca had called right as the bank was closing to tell her she needed to come in today.

Carolina stood and stretched, glad for a good night's sleep in a real bed.

She quickly slipped on her shoes and headed out into the backyard. She walked down by the lake with the dog at her side. She stopped and looked back at her house.

Her gaze traveled over the roof where the blue tarp covered the part of the roof that didn't have any shingles.

Thomas and Stanley had started taking the old roof off yesterday. They would throw off the old shingles in a pile on one side of the house. She wished he had brought some kind of dumpster instead of tossing it all on her lawn.

But he was the roofer and knew what he was doing so she didn't say anything to him about it.

She drank the last of her coffee and headed back inside to shower.

After her shower she put on some black pants and a light-blue sweater. She pulled on her black boots and glanced at her reflection in the mirror. The days were getting colder and she needed to remember to take her jacket with her when she went to town.

Carolina glanced at the time. She had time for a quick bowl of oatmeal before heading to the bank.

She headed into the kitchen. Black dog was lying in front of the unlit fireplace.

"I need to get someone out here to check the fireplace. I keep forgetting.," she muttered and pulled a pad and pencil out of the kitchen drawer and made a quick note. She also jotted down a reminder to buy some dog food. Perhaps she could ask around in town to see if anyone was missing a dog. Maybe Getty from the diner could help with that. She seemed to know everyone.

Carolina had finished her oatmeal when she heard pounding on the roof. She opened the back door to the deck and walked out and down the steps for a better view when something came flying at her.

She ducked just in time, barely missing a shingle coming for her head.

"Hey!" She yelled. "You almost hit me!"

"Are you crazy? Don't walk out here when you know we're working." Thomas peered his head over the top of the ridge of the roof and glared at her.

She bit back a sharp reply and stormed inside the house. Black dog tried to follow but she shook her head. "No. You stay outside. I'm leaving and don't want any accidents when I come back."

Grabbing her purse and her jacket she headed for her jeep.

CHAPTER 19

"*A*nd here's the last piece of paperwork to sign." Rebecca slid the contract across the desk.

Carolina took the pen and scribbled her name in the designated spot. She prayed she'd be able to get the loan paid back on time.

"Did Thomas start working on your roof?" Rebecca gathered the paperwork and straightened them into a neat pile before putting them in a folder.

"He started yesterday." Carolina pressed her lips into a thin line and then looked at her. "Can I ask you something?"

"Sure."

"How long has Stanley worked for Thomas?"

Rebecca grinned. "As long as I can remember. Why?"

"Well I'm just concerned. I mean he's an older man…"

"You're worried because he's an alcoholic."

Carolina gasped. "No! I mean...I wasn't going to say that."

"Well everyone knows. It's not a secret. Even Stanley will tell you if you ask him." She chortled.

Carolina leaned back in the chair, unsure how to proceed with the conversation.

"Carolina, if you are worried that Thomas won't do a good job, don't. He's been doing roofs and construction for as long as I've known him."

"How long has that been?"

"Since I was little. He may come across as rough around the edges but you just need to get to know him. You'll learn he can be trusted to do a good job."

"I don't think he's interested in anyone getting to know him."

"He is different with women than men. He was married once. And she died of cancer. He never remarried."

"Really?" Carolina suddenly felt compassion. He'd lost his wife to a terminal disease. She'd lost her marriage to another woman. They both knew the pain of losing someone they were supposed to grow old with. She let out a hefty sigh. "How sad."

"Yes. She was sick for such a long time. And there were so many treatments. It didn't help. He's still paying off her medical bills."

"I had no idea. That must mean he needs all the work he can get," she said softly.

Rebecca nodded. She took a drink of her coffee.

"Speaking of employment, have you started looking for a job?"

"Not yet. To be honest I'm not sure where to start. I was a housewife for twenty years. I don't think I have a lot to offer."

"Why don't you look into what your strengths are?" Rebecca offered. "Play up to that."

"What do you mean?"

"Are you a good cook? Did you decorate your house? What kinds of places did you volunteer?"

Carolina considered what her banker was saying. "I do cook, nothing fancy though. I had help decorating my house when we built it and I volunteered in the children's nursery. I really don't think any of those things can be turned into a profitable career, no matter how creative on paper."

Rebecca stood and gave her a reassuring smile. "Keep thinking about it. Something will fall into your lap. I have a feeling about these things."

She stood. "I hope so. Or else I'll be renting out rooms to earn money."

Rebecca sobered. "Hey, now that's an idea. You could have a B&B on the lake. Not only would it earn some money, you could have a lot of tax write-offs since it would be a business."

Carolina instantly resisted. "What if I get some crazy people? I don't know if that's the way for me to go." She hooked her purse on her arm. "I've got to go get some dog food." She cocked her head. "Hey, you don't know if someone lost a black dog by the lake, do you?"

"No, but I can post it on my social media account. If someone here has lost a dog then they will certainly be looking for it."

"Thank you. For everything." Carolina leaned across the desk and offered her hand. After they shook, she headed to her car and drove to the grocery store.

After getting groceries, she stopped in the diner to speak to Getty but learned it was her day off. The young waitress told her to come back tomorrow.

On the way home, Carolina thought about all that she needed. She needed to finish getting her house in shape and the expensive repairs completed. She needed to find Black Dog's owner. Most of all, she needed to get a job, and fast.

*a*knock woke Carolina up from a deep sleep. Black dog who was lying on the foot of her bed lifted his head and gave a single bark.

She sat up and looked over at the time on her phone.

Two a.m.

Fear suddenly grabbed her heart and squeezed. No one should be knocking on her door this late.

Screwing up her courage, she slung her legs over the side of the bed and wrapped the throw across her shoulders.

She crept slowly to the front door, her hands trembling. She quickly grabbed a flashlight off the the kitchen island. She'd found it in the laundry room when she'd been doing laundry and meant to put it by her bed.

The knocking was growing insistent.

"Go on boy," she whispered to the black dog, urging him to take the lead.

He peeked out carefully from behind her legs.

"Seriously? Some guard dog you are." She frowned at the dog and forced her feet to move toward the door.

She tried looking out but it was dark and the porch light had gone out.

"Who is it?" she called out, her voice shaking.

"Carolina Johnson, open this door immediately."

She frowned at the familiar voice.

"It can't be."

She unlocked and opened the door.

Standing on the other side was Janice Johnson, her ex-mother-in-law.

A curse word crawled up her throat but thankfully she held it in.

"Janice. What are you doing here?"

Janice lifted her chin and barged her way into the house. "What's the meaning of this? How dare you strand me?"

"Strand you?" She frowned. "What are you talking about?"

"I'm talking about the fact that I was coming to stay for a week with you and Chris. Imagine my surprise when I arrive at the house that's locked and no one is home. Thankfully, I had the address to the lake house." She walked inside and frowned. "What's going on here? Renovations? And when you are expecting company? That's really poor planning, Carolina."

Carolina narrowed her eyes at Janice. "Have you talked to your son recently?"

"No, where is he? Still asleep? Well, wake him up and tell him I'm here." She tossed her coat and expensive purse on the sofa.

"He's not here."

"Well, where in the world is he?"

"In Paris with his new wife." Carolina crossed her arms over her chest.

Janice spun around. Her eyes widened. "Excuse me?"

"You heard me. We are divorced. He married some twenty year-old. He got the house and I got the lake house in the divorce. They are currently on their honeymoon. Oh and she's pregnant. So there's that. I guess congratulations are in order." She rubbed her hand across her face.

Janice seemed to be taking in all the information.

"Look Janice, I'm sorry you drove all the way here to see your son. Clearly he's not here. And I don't know why he didn't call and let you know he would be traveling. It's late and I have a big day tomorrow. So you can either leave and get a hotel, or sleep on the couch."

"I've never slept on a couch in my entire life." She studied the large diamond on her well manicured hand. "It's too late to go into town. I'll sleep in the guest bedroom."

"Well, it's not fit for company."

"And why not?"

"Because I was left with a house that renters had

destroyed and I'm doing the best I can to rebuild it on very limited funds." She fired back.

"I think I need to call Chris."

"Perfect. I'm going to bed. There's bedding in the hall closet." She turned on her heel and headed into her bedroom shutting the door behind her.

The dog looked up at her.

"Things just got more complicated." She shook her head and climbed back into bed.

She couldn't fall back to sleep. She had never been on good terms with Janice. Her former mother-in-law had always thought her son could do no wrong and she constantly criticized Carolina when she came for a visit.

Janice always made her second-guess everything despite Carolina trying her best to please her.

Now she was tired and didn't have the energy to worry about it. She had enough things that were taking up her time.

Carolina closed her eyes and hoped that when she woke up in the morning Janice would be gone.

CHAPTER 21

*C*arolina woke up around six. She grabbed her throw and wrapped it around her shoulders.

She slipped her feet into her boots since she didn't have any slippers and went into the kitchen to grab some coffee.

Janice was sitting on the edge of the couch stiff as a board. She could almost pass for a mannequin.

"Good morning." Carolina passed her on her way into the kitchen. She was kind of surprised she was still here.

"I didn't sleep a wink," her former mother-in-law reported, sounding as stiff as she looked. She didn't bother looking at Carolina as she spoke.

"Sorry to hear that. Would you like some coffee before you go?"

"Coffee and cream." She didn't bother moving but kept her position on the couch.

Carolina fixed two cups of coffee and handed one

to her. "I'm going to sit outside. You're welcome to join me."

Janice looked at her like she was crazy. "It's freezing outside."

"I know but the dog has to go outside and I like watching the sunrise." Carolina headed to the back door.

Janice began telling her reasons why she shouldn't go outside this early in the morning, but Carolina ignored her and stepped outside anyway.

The wind was colder and she was grateful for her boots but wished she had worn her coat.

"Hurry up. Go do your business," she told the black dog.

He took his time sniffing each dead blade of grass before finally finding a suitable spot.

When he was finished, she reached for the doorknob and glanced over her shoulder. "Are you coming in?"

The dog looked at her and then headed toward the closest neighbor's house.

She couldn't blame him. Even a canine could sense the trouble inside.

Carolina sighed, realizing she was going to have to face her former mother-in-law alone.

She stepped inside, grateful for the warmth. Janice was aiming a remote at the fireplace.

"This thing doesn't work."

"That's because it's a TV remote." Carolina headed into the kitchen.

Janice looked around, "I don't see a TV."

"That's because the renters stole it along with the dryer and other items."

"Why did you let that happen?" Janice demanded.

"I didn't let anything happen. I had no idea who Chris was renting the lake house to. Apparently, they were causing trouble on the lake because one of them ran over someone's mailbox and was disturbing the peace."

Janice arched her brow. "You should have had a better handle on who you rented it to."

All the emotions she had been storing up deep inside rose like a rolling boil into the back of her throat. She slammed her coffee mug down on the kitchen counter and spun around.

"Like everything else in my life I didn't know what was going on because Chris kept me in the dark. I had no idea who was renting the lake house because every time I asked, he told me it was none of my business. And I had no idea that he was cheating on me for over a year because he said he was working extra hours at the hospital. And I had no idea he'd gotten his twenty-two-year old mistress pregnant until she showed up at a neighbor's party and announced it. I didn't ask for any of these things, yet here I am dealing with the fallout. All my life you have done nothing but criticize me and tell me I wasn't enough. Well congratulations, you don't have to concern your-self any longer. You are done with me. You now have a new daughter-in-law that I'm sure will please you in every way. Now if you don't mind I've got to get ready."

Janice stared at her like she'd grown a third head. "Where are you going?"

"I've got to go into town to try and find a job so I can pay back the loan for this roof I'm having put on." She didn't wait around to hear anymore of what Janice had to say.

With adrenaline pumping through her veins, she stormed into the bathroom.

CHAPTER 22

*W*hen Carolina came out dressed in tan slacks and a white button-down shirt, Janice was nowhere to be seen.

She let out a sigh of relief. She felt bad about speaking to her former mother-in-law that way, but it had been a long time coming. Frankly, it felt good to put her in her place.

She had read the story of Ruth in the Bible and wondered what it would be like to have a mother-in-law who truly loved you. Ruth had been willing to give up everything to follow her mother-in-law and in the end she'd been blessed.

Carolina never had that kind of relationship with Janice. Even from the get-go the woman made it clear that she didn't think Carolina was good enough for her son.

Janice's husband had died before Carolina came into the picture. From what Chris had told her the couple had been married almost fifty years before he had a massive heart attack.

She'd always thought that Janice was jealous of Carolina for taking Chris away. Instead of seeing it as gaining a daughter she saw it as losing a son.

No matter. It wasn't her problem now. She bet Janice would get on well with Kylie. She was young enough, thin enough, and now soon to be mother of Chris's baby.

The thought cut through her like a knife.

Something inside her wasn't surprised though. All her life there was some tiny voice in the back of her head that told her she wasn't worthy of the life she led.

And now it had come true.

She shook her head and slid into her jeep. As she drove into town, she took time to notice all the trees changing colors.

It felt more beautiful here, even with all the issues she was having.

Her stomach rumbled reminding her she had been so eager to get away from Janice that she'd forgotten to eat.

She spotted the diner and found an empty spot in front and parked. She could get a quick breakfast and maybe talk to Getty about some job opportunities.

She walked in and saw that someone had left a copy of the newspaper on top of the garbage can. She grabbed it and and located an empty table in the corner of the room. She sat and pulled out her notebook and pen.

She wrote the word, jobs at the top of the page and turned to the classifieds.

"Hey Carolina." Getty walked up and poured her a fresh cup of coffee. She pulled out some tiny tubs of cream and packets of sugar out of her apron and placed it beside the cup. "Cream and sugar, right?"

"Yes. How did you remember?"

"Oh, it's part of the job. Shelly told me you came in yesterday looking for me. Can I help you with something?" Her gaze landed on her notebook.

"I hope so. First of all you don't happen to know if anyone lost a black dog out by the lake do you?"

Getty shook her head. "I haven't heard anyone report a lost dog. But I do know that people will dump unwanted pets of theirs hoping someone will take them in."

Carolina frowned. "That's so sad."

"Yeah I know. I can't imagine dumping a poor animal just because you're tired of them."

Carolina nodded. She felt very much like the black dog.

Getty put another paper napkin down on the table. "Was that all you wanted to ask?"

"Well, no. You see, I need to get a job and I was wondering if you needed any help here.

"Sorry hon. We are fully staffed." Getty grinned. "Besides you don't look like a waitress."

"Yeah? What do I look like?" Carolina smiled and cupped her face in her hands giving Getty her full attention.

"Well, you look like director of a charity or an entrepreneur."

"Really?" Her eyes grew wide and then she burst out into a laugh. "I am as far from an entrepreneur as is possible."

"What are you good at?"

She sighed. "I have no idea. I was a housewife for years. It's all I've done."

"Oh, hon, I'm sure you're not giving yourself much credit. Being a housewife was hard. I did it before my husband died."

"Oh, I'm sorry. I didn't know you lost your husband."

"He's been gone for about ten years. You get used to the silence but not used to being lonely." She blinked away emotion and then shook her head. "Look at me being all chatty. What can I get you for breakfast?"

"Oh," Carolina grabbed a menu and took a quick glance. "I'm not really hungry."

"Well, you need to eat. You are much too skinny."

She laughed. "I've never been called skinny."

Getty gave her a curious look. "How about an everything omelet?"

"What's in it?"

"Everything."

"Perfect, I'll have that."

Getty smiled and went to put her order in.

Carolina took a sip of her coffee and glanced through the want ads. Her options were limited in the small town.

Welder. Mechanic. Nurse. Teacher.

All those things required a degree or training.

She sighed and glanced at the potted plant on the ledge above her. The leaves were turning brown and it looked like it was about to die. She stuck her finger in the pot. Her finger sunk into soggy dirt.

Getty returned and placed her breakfast in front of her. "I don't know what's wrong with that plant. I keep watering it but it seems like it's destined to die."

"This kind of plant needs more sun and less water." Carolina picked up the plant and carried the pot to the window. She set it right where the sunlight was beaming in.

She returned to her booth and grabbed her napkin.

Getty gave her a strange look. "How did you know that?"

"Oh, I love plants. That's the one thing I really need to do to the lake house. Put some flowers in my flowerbed. " She gave her a wistful look. "I bet my mums are in full bloom right now. I planted them near my dining room window so I could see them when we ate dinner."

Getty's hand slapped the table.

Carolina jumped.

"That's it. That's what you need to do."

"What?" Carolina frowned clearly confused.

"Landscape. Why, the owner of the landscape business, Green Thumb Nursery needs help. She's an older lady and all her summer help went back to school."

"Really?" Carolina cocked her head. "People normally landscape their homes in springtime."

"That may be true. But around here, especially around the lake, people love doing up their flowerbeds and porches for Halloween and Thanksgiving." Getty pulled off a piece of paper from her pad and scribbled. "Here's her address. Go over there after you finish breakfast. I'm going to give her a call and tell her that I'm sending you over."

"Really?" For the first time since arriving, her hopes lifted.

"Yes." Getty patted her arm. "See, everything works out like it should."

"I hope so." She picked up her fork and dug into her omelet. The ingredients blended together in a wonderful medley and made her mouth water for more.

"This is wonderful." Carolina's eyes closed in pleasure.

"Glad you like it." Getty sobered. "Oh and hun?"

"Yes?"

"The owner is an older woman, kind of set in her ways. But don't worry. Her bark is far worse than her bite." Getty nodded encouragingly.

"I'll remember that." She smiled. After dealing with her former mother-in-law, she could take on anyone.

CHAPTER 23

*C*arolina pulled up to the landscape business. The building was in need of paint and the sign out front had two missing letters. Lining the cracked sidewalk under the window that was in bad need of a washing, the summer plants were starting to die and the mums needed desperate attention. She saw some pumpkins and small hay bales off to the side but they were not arranged in any kind of presentation.

She slid out of her jeep and walked over to the area with the stone and rock. The owner had a nice assortment but she could do more to draw attention to her merchandise.

"I'll be with you in a minute." A woman called out from behind the building.

"Take your time." Carolina returned the greeting and spotted the large greenhouses. She made her way over to the first one and peeked inside.

There were evergreens in all shapes and sizes and

near the back were some asparagus ferns probably left over from the summer.

She exited that building and went into the next greenhouse. This time she smiled when she stepped inside. The three large tables were overflowing with mums in shades of yellow, red, orange, and burgundy. She was surprised to see so many inside and not set outside to showcase the merchandise.

Carolina proceeded into the third building which housed a table of pumpkins, again all shapes and sizes, and a table of poinsettias along with miniature Christmas trees.

Someone behind her cleared their throat. "Can I help you?"

Carolina smiled and turned. "Yes I am…" Her heart lurched. Her smile faded.

The air left her lungs.

She may have handled her former mother-in-law but standing before her was the neighbor that hated her.

"You." Bernice narrowed her eyes. "What are you doing here?"

"I …um…" She clasped her hands together and fought for words.

Carolina cleared her throat from the lump that had appeared. Now was not the time to back down. She was out of options.

"I'm here because Getty at the diner said you were looking for help."

Bernice looked shocked.

"You? You're looking to work here?" She blinked.

"Well, yes. I don't have professional experience but I have personally redone our flowerbeds at our... I mean at my old home many times before. And I'm good with houseplants."

Bernice snorted. "Well, you need to do something about the flowerbeds at the lake house."

"I know. And I will. Once I get some money coming in." She lifted her head, determined not to waver in her determination.

Bernice shook her head and walked over to the wheelbarrow. She began loading pumpkins.

Carolina swallowed her pride and began helping her.

"What are you doing?"

"I'm trying to get a job."

Bernice stopped what she was doing and straightened. "Why do you want this job so badly?"

"Because it's the only thing I'm good at."

"What did you do before?"

"I was a housewife. And apparently not very good at that either since my husband dumped me." She looked away embarrassed by her verbal diarrhea.

Bernice snorted. "I wouldn't give much credence to what a man thought about me." She bent and picked up a Cinderella pumpkin.

Carolina swallowed and looked at the woman.

"It's manual work. You'll ruin your manicure." She glanced at Carolina's hands.

"I don't care."

"I pay twenty-five an hour. I am closed on Sunday and Mondays. And only open half a day on Thursday. Work hours are eight to five, except on Saturdays and we are open until six."

She nodded. "Okay. So does that mean I have the job?"

"It means I'll give you a trial period."

"Thank you. I can start tomorrow."

"You better. You still need to pay for my vet bill."

CHAPTER 24

*C*arolina arrived home after five. Bernice had made her start working that same day which was not convenient given she was wearing black slacks and leather boots, not exactly work clothes. She stood at her front door and toed the leather boots off. She would have to get some rubber boots to work in.

She smiled when she noticed Janice's car was gone.

"Where have you been?" Thomas rounded the corner of the house.

"I was in town where I got a job. I started today."

He scowled as his gaze roamed up and down her body. "You're dirty."

"I bet you talk to all the ladies like that."

He ignored her sarcasm and continued to examine her clothes with disdain. "Where did you find a job? Mucking out horse stalls?"

"Your confidence in me is making me blush." She glared. "I started working at Green Thumb Nursery."

He blinked. "But Bernice Stacks owns it."

"Yes. And she actually hired me." She held up her hand. "I know I know it's hard to believe considering how much she hates me. I guess what she dislikes more is not having employees. Besides, this way she knows I'll have the money for her vet bill that she keeps threatening me with."

After getting her leather boots off she propped them up by the door and reached inside her purse for her keys.

"Did you make good progress with the roof today?" she asked while searching for her keys.

"Not really. Stanley fell off the roof."

She spun around and grabbed his arm. "Oh my gosh is he okay? Did you call an ambulance?"

Thomas scowled. "He's fine. He got into a bottle of whiskey late last night. He arrived here before I did, still drunk, and was on the roof crowing like a rooster. I startled him when I climbed up the ladder and caused him to fall. He's fine but he just about gave me a heart attack."

Carolina let out the breath she'd been holding. "I'm glad he's okay. Do you really think he should be on the roof anyway? He's a lot older."

He rubbed the back of his neck. Though he was scowling, Carolina could see the worry in his eyes. "Working helps keep him occupied. When he's occupied he's not thinking about drinking. I thought I was helping him by giving him a job, but maybe you're right."

"It's hard to watch someone make bad mistakes over and over again. In the end people have to make up their minds to change." As she spoke the words, she realized it pertained to her as well. "But thank God he's okay and not seriously hurt."

"Don't thank Him yet. There's rain in the forecast and I'm a man down."

"Is there anyone else you can hire?"

"No."

"But that other roofer had a ton of workers when he came. I bet…"

"He had a ton of workers because he cons minorities to work for him. He hardly pays them anything and when they try to leave, he threatens to call immigration on them."

"Are you serious? I never would have pegged him to be so underhanded."

"You need to learn to read people's character."

Carolina let out a huff. "Well I hired you. What does that say about my judge of character?"

He blinked. "It only proves my point."

She barked out a laugh.

In return he stared at her strangely.

Carolina sobered. "Sorry I wasn't home today. If I knew I was going to start working today I would have left the back door unlocked so you could have access to something to drink." She stepped inside. "Come inside and I'll get you some cold water."

"Thanks." He bent and pulled off his boots before stepping inside.

"Go on in the kitchen I need to get out of these muddy clothes first." She headed to the bedroom and shut the door. She quickly changed into some yoga pants and a sweatshirt and some thick socks.

When she walked into the living room, Thomas was standing by the fireplace looking up into the chimney.

"I don't suppose you know anyone who can take a look at that for me? I'd like to make sure it works before I use it. The last thing I need is to burn the house down. Because judging by the way my life is going, it's a total possibility."

"It just needs cleaning. It's a real wood burning fireplace, no gas starter." He looked at her. "Have you ever made a fire before?"

"No. When we bought the lake house I was hoping we would get to use it on the weekends. But my husband, ex-husband, decided to rent it out. I think he didn't want to use it because it wasn't new. He tends to like new things. And new people." She sneered and went to the kitchen. She pulled out some bottled waters and handed one to him.

She pulled out the pot roast from last night and set it on the counter.

"You made that just for you?"

"I did. But it's too much. I'll fix you a plate if you're hungry. It's the least I can do since I stranded you outside all day without the use of a bathroom or water."

"I'm used to it. The clients I get don't allow me in the house."

"That's pretty rude." She pulled down some of her plates she recently bought and began loading them with roast beef. She added some leftover mashed potatoes as well.

"I don't have any cornbread or rolls. But I do have crackers."

"Crackers are fine." He sat down at the small island and watched her as she worked.

"I would invite you to the dining room, but since I don't have any furniture, this will have to do." She warmed up his food before she set his plate before him at the kitchen island.

"You always eat at the dining room table?" He picked up his fork.

"I used to." Her mind turned to memories of dinner when she was married. She always had a good meal ready for Chris when he got off work. "We used to eat at the dining room table all the time. Then he started taking his plate into the living room so he could watch TV while he ate. I guess I should have known something was going on when he stopped communicating."

He took a bite of the roast beef. "He sounds like an idiot. Any man who would leave a woman that can cook like this isn't right in the head."

Carolina smiled. "I think you're right." She picked up her fork and began eating.

"This is really good. I've not had pot roast in…well I can't remember when."

"I don't normally cook like this just for myself. I guess old habits die hard."

"Don't let them. You don't stop living just because that part of your life stopped. If you do then you'll find yourself struggling to get through the day. Just getting by is no way to live."

Curious she took a sip of water. "Is that what you do? Just get by?"

His fork halted in midair. He lifted his gaze to her. His eyes shadowed in pain.

"Sorry. I didn't meant to pry."

He lowered his fork to his plate. "I lost my wife to cancer."

"I'm so sorry. That must have been really hard." She reached over and laid her hand on his arm.

He glanced down at her touch but didn't move away.

"It's been five years now. We were married for fifteen years and then one day she found out she had cancer during a routine checkup."

Carolina nodded slowly. "It's sobering how life can change on a dime."

"Yeah it is." He shook his head and picked up his fork. "So what are your plans for the future?"

"Future?" She chortled. "I really haven't thought about a future."

"You're still young. You have a future."

"Thanks for saying that but I'm forty. I'm no spring chicken." She shrugged.

"You don't look your age. I figured you to be thirty-three or thirty-five."

"Thank you." She ducked her head a little unsure

how to take the compliment. "What about you? What are your future plans?"

"Work until I can retire. I have a plot of land here on the lake. Had it for years. We were planning on building our lake house but when Lilly passed, I didn't really think about it anymore."

"Do you live nearby?"

"I live on the other side of town on twenty acres. I have my shop out there too."

"Have you always been a roofer?"

Thomas nodded. "I'm actually a licensed contractor. I used to build houses until the other younger contracters priced me out of jobs. So, I got my roofer's license. My only competition is Randy."

"Sounds like you two are very competitive."

He grinned a little. "We are. He used to date Lilly before we got married."

"Really?" She gasped, understanding the animosity between them. "No wonder he tries to steal your business."

"No doubt." He chuckled.

She'd never heard him laugh before. It was a nice laugh.

"So can you clean my fireplace if I pay you?"

"Sure. I'll look at it tomorrow when I'm on the roof. I may be an hour late tomorrow. I have to run by and check on Stanley and bring him something to eat."

"Maybe you should take him the rest of this roast beef. Like I said, there's plenty. I'll fix you up a big plate before you go."

"I'm sure he would appreciate it. Thank you."

"It's the least I can do since he fell off my roof." She cringed at the thought of what might have happened.

He scratched his head. "In fact, I think he wasn't hurt because he was so relaxed. It even kind of looked like he bounced when he hit the ground."

She looked at him and then burst out laughing. He cracked a grin and then barked out a laugh as well.

Their laughter swelled until she had tears rolling down her eyes. Catching her breath she wiped the tears with her fingertips.

"I haven't laughed that hard in a long time. Thanks for that mental image." She smiled.

"We all need a laugh every now and then," he agreed. He stood up and took his plate to the sink and washed it off.

"Just leave it in the sink," she told him. "I'm sorry I don't have any dessert."

Thomas patted his stomach. "I'm stuffed. I couldn't eat another bite. It was good. Been awhile since I had a homecooked meal. Thank you."

"Thanks for joining me. It's nice to have company for dinner." Something about sharing a meal made her feel a little less sad about her situation in life.

She pulled out a plastic container and lid. She filled it up with roast beef and mashed potatoes.

"Take this to Stanley. Tell him I hope he gets better soon."

"I wouldn't worry about Stanley. He's enjoying his time off. He's binge-watching Family Feud." He took the container she held out to him. "Thanks for this. I'm sure he'll enjoy it."

She walked him to the door. When she opened it, the black dog was sitting there waiting for her.

Thomas laughed. "Here's your friend. Have you given him a name yet?"

"No. I keep thinking he belongs to someone and they'll show up for him."

"I wouldn't count on it. Go ahead and name him. I'm pretty sure he's your dog now."

"I suppose so. I guess I'll have to come up with a name." She bit her lip.

"Don't overthink it." He looked at her.

"Okay, well how about Phoenix?"

"Like a phoenix rising?"

"Yeah. Maybe we are both getting a new beginning. You know, rising from the ashes."

CHAPTER 25

*C*arolina woke early the next day. It was Thursday which meant a half day at the nursery. She had run some decorating ideas by Bernice, to make people more apt to get their landscape and front porch decorated for fall.

The old lady narrowed her eyes at her. "I don't think that will help sales. People don't decorate much in the fall."

"But they do," Carolina argued. "Some of the lake house owners put out some really cute porch décor."

Bernice waved her off. "You should take some of your own advice and decorate your house. It's becoming an eyesore."

She sighed and reminded her boss. "It's on my list to do. Once I get some extra funds."

"Didn't you get alimony in the divorce?" She pointed her trowel at her. She'd been repotting a miniature Christmas tree that had outgrown its container.

"I did. But I don't know if it's going to be on time. It's hard to put my trust in that."

Bernice waved the trowel in the air. "Don't ever trust a man to make good on his promise. They're all snakes."

"All of them?"

"Yes, all of them."

Maybe Bernice was right.

"We only have a few more minutes before we close and we need to move these pumpkins inside. We've got some mischievous kids that like to steal them."

"Really? I had no idea. I'll get the wheelbarrow." She pointed to a group of dying mums under a tree. "What are you going to do with those?"

"Dump them. I got too many in and those didn't get my attention."

"Do you mind if I take them?"

Bernice lifted her eyebrows. "Take them home? To plant?"

"Yeah. Maybe I can get them to grow. I was going to buy some of your pumpkins and those ferns as well. Maybe someone driving by will see and ask who did it. I can refer your business."

Bernice barked out a laugh. "You may be good with plants but no one is *that* good. Take all those dying mums and the ferns. It saves me the energy from throwing them away. And I'll sell you the pumpkins at cost."

She smiled. "Great."

"But there's no way you are going to make a success out of those. They are too far gone."

"Maybe. But I think they just need a second chance and some love."

Bernice snarled and walked away.

Carolina quickly finished her work and then as soon as the business closed, she paid for the pumpkins and began loading everything into the back of her jeep. If she thought Bernice would offer to help she was sadly mistaken. After locking up the building she headed for her jeep.

She changed from her rubber boots, which she'd bought on sale at the farmer supply store and slid on her old sneakers before getting into her car.

Driving through town she spotted a yard sale. An old gray watering can caught her attention so she pulled over and got out.

Her mind started to spin with ideas for decorating as she picked up the watering can.

She glanced around for its owner, finally spotting a young woman, her arms filled with a baby. "I don't see a price on this."

The owner smiled. "It's old and does have a leak. We found it in the attic when we bought the house. How about five dollars?"

"I'll take it." Carolina pulled some money out of her purse. Her gaze swept across the items lined up on the driveway. "Looks like you have some good items here."

"I'm hoping it does well. I am not moving that stuff back inside." She laughed and the baby flailed his arms.

Carolina's gaze stopped on a worn wicker basket and three legged stool. She walked over. "How much for both of these?"

"I don't know. Ten for both?"

Carolina's eyes widened. "You're asking too little. But I'm not one to turn down such a great price." She handed the woman the money.

Satisfied with her purchases, she took her items back to the car and loaded them.

She glanced at the time on her watch and decided to stop at the grocery store.

Her appetite was returning and she had a craving for some chili for dinner.

When she pulled into her driveway she noticed that Thomas had managed to get all the old shingles off and was now in the process of prepping the roof for the new shingles.

He was making pretty good progress despite the fact he was working solo.

She grabbed her groceries and headed inside. Once she put everything away, she went back outside.

She shielded her eyes against the bright sun and looked up at Thomas. "How's it going?"

"It's going."

"I stopped by the sandwich store beside the grocery and grabbed a couple of sandwiches for lunch. I have an extra one if you are hungry."

He frowned and glanced at the time on his watch. "I

guess I worked through lunch. I'll take you up on your offer. Be down in a minute."

She nodded and opened the back of her jeep and began unloading.

"What's all this for?" Thomas appeared at her elbow.

"I'm going to decorate the door and flower beds."

"I hate to tell you but Bernice ripped you off. Those plants are dead."

She scowled. "They're not dead. They still have life in them. They just need some attention."

He snorted. "I wouldn't take that to the bank. I still say Bernice ripped you off."

"Actually she gave me the plants for free and I paid for the pumpkins." She shrugged.

"She must like you if she gave you something free."

"Trust me she doesn't like me. She reminded me this morning when I arrived about paying for her cat's vet bill."

Thomas let out a laugh. "That's Bernice alright. Never lets anything go." He carried two pumpkins to the front door and set them down. Phoenix appeared from the back of the house and went over to sniff the pumpkins.

"Hey Phoenix. Has he been here all day?"

"This is the first time I've seen him. I looked when I drove into the neighborhood but didn't spot him at anyone's house. I'm afraid he's yours for life."

As if sensing they were talking about him, Phoenix lifted his head and looked at them both.

She set down her mums and scratched him between the ears. "That's okay. I'll keep him."

"He seems smart enough. He'll be good protection for you at night."

"I hope I won't need to have any protection. I mean it's pretty safe out here, right?"

Thomas pulled a hankerchief out of the back of his pocket and wiped his hands. "There was a break-in about a year ago but they found out it was someone passing through. But it is usually quiet out here."

After unloading everything, Thomas went into the bathroom to wash up while she set out the sandwiches.

"That looks good. I forgot how hungry I was." He rested his hand on his stomach.

"Good, eat up." She handed him a paper plate with a club sandwich and some chopped apple. She grabbed the pitcher out of the refrigerator and poured them both some tea.

"Want to sit outside?" She asked. "I know it's chilly but I hate not enjoying the outdoors while I can. Winter will be here soon enough."

He held the back door open while she walked outside. They sat around the small table on the deck.

"Your's is one of the few houses with a boat launch. But I don't see the boat."

Carolina sighed. "Apparently Chris sold it. I didn't find out about it until the divorce."

"Sounds like you didn't communicate well."

"You would be right. You're lucky that you had a

good marriage. I had always thought that I didn't deserve the kind of life I found myself in."

"What do you mean?" He gave her a quizzical look.

"I mean, Chris came from a wealthy family, he was handsome, smart, made friends easily. He became a doctor and did well for himself." She shrugged and picked at the lettuce. "I always was kind of waiting for the other shoe to drop. For God to realize that I didn't deserve that kind of lifestyle."

"Didn't deserve?"

"Yeah. We are total opposites. My family didn't have much money. I mean I was happy and had a safe home, my parents loved me. We might not have had vacations every summer but we always had picnics at my grandparent's farm under a large oak tree." She nodded at the tree in the back yard. "Just like that one. I'd love to have a large wooden table underneath those limbs for dinners and picnics."

He studied her intently. "Did you realize your marriage was in trouble? Did you see it coming?"

She sighed. "When I look back on everything, I do. But when I was in the middle of it, I didn't. Chris started coming home later and later. We didn't talk much when he did. I always figured he was tired. I didn't realize he was tired because he had a twenty-two year-old girlfriend." She took a drink. "The shocking part was none of my friends told me what was going on. Now I can see they all knew. I think that's what hurt the most."

"Doesn't sound like they were real friends."

"Maybe they just didn't want to get involved." She took a bite and looked out over the lake.

"That's what real friends do. They get involved. Even if it's messy, but they damn sure don't leave you."

She sat there stunned, not sure what to say. His words rang true but at the same time, she couldn't accept them.

"Hello? Carolina? Where are you?" A voice called out in the house.

Carolina felt the blood drain from her face. "Dear God no."

"Who is it?" He stood and looked at her.

"My former mother-in-law."

CHAPTER 26

*T*homas followed Carolina inside. Janice stood in the middle of the living room.

Carolina frowned. "Janice, what are you doing here?"

"I called Chris on my way back to his house. He told me he and his wife were in Paris and didn't expect to be home for weeks." She looked more than a little put out.

Carolina crossed her arms over her chest. "That still doesn't explain why you are *here*."

"He wouldn't give me the code to open his house so I could stay there," her former mother-in-law explained.

"Why not?" Carolina looked over her shoulder. Thomas was standing there sizing up Janice.

Janice spotted Thomas and narrowed her eyes. "Who is that?"

"This is Thomas Harding. He's the one putting a

roof on the house."

Thomas didn't offer a greeting so Carolina turned her attention back to Janice. "If you came back here to get a key to the house it won't do you any good. Chris changed the locks while we were in court."

"I'm not here to get a key. I'm here to stay with you until Chris comes back."

"What?" She gasped.

"I'll take the spare bedroom." She picked up the luggage by the door that had escaped Carolina's attention. "Just point me in the direction."

Carolina was so stunned she couldn't speak.

"Never mind I'll find it." Janice marched off down the hallway to one of the guest bedrooms.

"I'm guessing this is a surprise." Thomas said.

She spun around. "I don't understand. She hates me. Why would she want to stay here? Why doesn't she go to a hotel?"

Thomas slowly folded his arms across his chest. "I'm sure she doesn't hate you."

"She gave me a girdle for Christmas one year. I'm pretty sure she hates me."

Thomas gave her a horrific look. "You're kidding, right?"

She shook her head and motioned for Thomas to follow her outside and then closed the door behind them. "I don't get it. This makes no sense to me at all."

He cocked his head. "Think she's trying to start trouble?"

"Thomas, that woman is nothing but trouble.

Maybe she's staying to spy on me. Maybe she thinks I have something that Chris didn't get in the divorce." She shook her head and glanced down at her hand.

"That's it. She's here to get my engagement ring. It belonged to Janice's mother."

Thomas's gaze dropped to her hand. "I've been meaning to ask why you are still wearing it."

"Habit I suppose," she shrugged and twisted the ring on her finger.

"I will see if she asks for it back. In the meantime, I'll give her the number to the motel in town." Thomas turned and headed down the stairs. "Thanks for the sandwich. I've got to get back to work in order to stay on schedule."

CHAPTER 27

*C*arolina took a deep breath, paused in front of the open door to the guest room trying to gather courage to face the situation. She straightened her shoulders and marched in. "Janice, we need to talk."

Janice looked up from unpacking her suitcase. Without responding she hung a shirt on a hanger and placed it in the closet.

Carolina propped her hands on her hips. "Janice, did you hear me? I don't think your staying is a good idea. As you can see, this room doesn't even have a bed."

"Yes, what happened to it? I know when you and Chris bought the house you had it furnished."

"I'm guessing the renters stole it. I've already had to replace some things. And I don't have the money right now to get a bed in here for you to sleep on. In fact," she took the shirt she just hung up and handed it back to her, "I believe you will be more comfortable at the motel in town."

"Motel?" Janice huffed. "I've never stayed at a motel in all my life."

"Well, there's a first time for everything isn't there?" She forced a smile.

Janice narrowed her eyes. "I'd much prefer to stay here. If you don't mind." She snatched the shirt out of Carolina's hand and hung it back up.

Carolina didn't have time for this crap. She considered standing her ground when she noticed a look cross Janice's face. Was that...fear?

"Whatever. There's tea in the refrigerator and half a sandwich in there too. I've got to get busy outside." She turned and walked down the hall.

Janice followed after her. "Where are you going? Are you not going to get me settled in my bedroom? What about a bed? Or mattress at least?"

Carolina sighed and turned around. "Janice, I just bought a new mattress and used bed frame for my bedroom. I don't have the funds to replace everything right now." She kept walking right out the front door.

Outside she shoved her fingers through her hair and looked at the dying mums and bright orange pumpkins sitting near her door. She went to her jeep and pulled out the work gloves and rubber boots and quickly changed.

She needed to feel dirt beneath her hands and wind in her hair to help her forget that horrible woman who had made her life hell for so long. Why in the world did she believe she had the right to just march in and make herself comfortable without an invite?

Of course, there was another issue to consider. Janice wouldn't stay long in her house.

It wasn't new enough for her snobby expectations.

Carolina worked with an energy she didn't know she had. She had gone to the small shed off to the side of the house to retrieve a shovel and realized all the tools were gone. Thankfully Thomas had a shovel in the bed of his truck that he allowed her to borrow.

Despite the hard ground, she made quick work of the flowerbeds. She planted a lot of the mums while putting two of the hardiest looking mums into small planters she found in the shed. She planted the ferns in two tall planters and arranged pumpkins around them and the front door.

She grabbed some small limbs and twigs and made a quick arrangement in the watering can and used it as part of the décor. She propped the wicker basket by the front door and retrieved a red and black flannel blanket from the laundry room and draped it over the edge of the basket. She removed the dead debris from the flowerbeds and trimmed back the evergreen with some hand shears that Thomas lent her.

She wiped the sweat from her forehead as she examined her work.

"That's quite a difference." Thomas came up behind her.

"Yeah. It certainly needed it." She looked at the

setting sun. "Wow I didn't realize it had gotten so late. I'm making chili tonight. Want to stay and eat?"

"Are you kidding? Not with dragon lady inside."

She barked out a laugh and handed him his shovel. "I completely understand. I'm willing to bet she'll be gone by tomorrow."

"Good luck in the meantime." He loaded his shovel in the back of the truck and slid inside. She went to her jeep and pulled off her rubber boots and work gloves and placed them in the back, before walking up to the front door.

She stepped inside and froze.

CHAPTER 28

*J*anice was putting some limbs in the fireplace. She bent down and struck a match.

"What are you doing?" Carolina hollered as she ran over and blew out the match.

"I'm building a fire. It's freezing in here. Besides I like a fire when it's cold outside."

"You can't build a fire until the fireplace has been checked out and cleaned. Otherwise you might burn the whole house down." She pointed to the wood. "Where did you get that wood?"

"In the backyard."

Carolina scowled. "There wasn't any wood lying around in the backyard."

"I sawed it off the tree. I found a handsaw outside."

She took three deep cleansing breaths before attempting to speak. "This wood is still green. You can't burn that kind of wood. It will smoke up the house too much. Besides, cutting those limbs off might hurt my tree."

"Well, how was I supposed to know? I'm not used to doing manual labor." Janice lifted her chin and shoved her platinum blond hair away from her eyes. "You know, you were much more enjoyable to be around when you were married to my son. Now, you're so bitter."

Shock ricocheted through her body.

Was she turning into a bitter woman?

She really wanted to tell Janice what she thought of her but that would only confirm Janice's opinion of her and she wasn't going to give her the satisfaction.

"When are we going out for dinner?" Janice brushed her hands off on the kitchen towel she found on the island.

"We are not going out for dinner. I'm making chili." She went into the kitchen and washed her hands.

"I don't want chili. I want a nice steak."

"Why don't you go into town? I'm sure there are some wonderful restaurants that have a nice steak on the menu."

"Go by myself?"

"Sure, why not?"

"Why, I've never dined by myself. Only rejects dine by themselves."

Carolina spun around, anger pulsing in her veins. "I've dined by myself. Are you saying I'm a reject?" The voice of her mother reminding her of the fruits of the Spirit played in her head, especially love and patience.

Those two attributes were hard to practice when it came to being around Janice.

"I, uh, I..." Janice stuttered trying to find her words.

"You know what, Janice? Never mind. I'm going to take a hot bath and then cook dinner. Don't burn the house down in the meantime." She stormed off into her room locking the door behind her.

CHAPTER 29

*C*arolina stayed in the tub until her fingers were wrinkled and the water was cold. She got out of the tub and quickly toweled off and changed. Maybe when she went out into the living room Janice would be gone.

She opened the door to find Phoenix was sitting there waiting for her.

"How'd you get inside?" She cocked her head.

"He was scratching at the door." Janice had Carolina's throw from the couch wrapped around her shoulders.

"You let him in?" Carolina gaped. Janice hated animals. Especially large dogs who did not have a pedigree.

"He was going to scratch the glass if I didn't." She narrowed her eyes on the dog.

"Are you hungry?" She walked into the kitchen.

"Starving." Janice followed her.

"Great. I'll get the chili ready."

"I forgot my acid reflux medication." She huffed.

"There may be some in the cabinet over the sink." Carolina would check herself but she had her hands full of ground beef.

Janice went through the cabinets to no avail. "Nothing."

"I don't make my chili spicy so maybe it won't bother you."

"I've never had your chili before." Janice lifted her chin. "Chris usually cooks me a nice filet when I'm there."

Carolina bit back a reply and focused on browning the meat. She added some garlic salt while it simmered.

"Where did you find that dog? He looks awful. He is nothing but skin and bones." Janice reluctantly sat on the barstool.

"He just showed up. I asked around but I think someone just dumped him." Carolina pulled out a couple of cans of crushed tomatoes and a large pot.

"I don't blame them. He's no good to anyone in his condition."

Carolina stiffened. She put the spatula down and cut her eyes at her. "You would throw away an animal because he's too old?"

"That's not what I said." She crossed her arms over her chest.

"Janice…" She was interrupted by Janice's ringing phone.

Janice looked at who was calling and smiled. "Hello

151

darling." She slid off the stool and walked into the living room for privacy.

Carolina strained to hear who she was talking to, but couldn't make out the conversation.

It was probably Chris calling to tell her what an awful wife Carolina had been and he had traded up with Kylie.

She wished Janice would just leave her in peace. She was so different from her own mother. Where Janice was materialistic and cared about keeping up appearances, her own mother had been satisfied with the simple life of living on a farm and helping out where she could.

Despite how hard it was to like Janice, Carolina still couldn't bring herself to actually kick the woman out. She couldn't understand why Janice was here anyway. Probably just to annoy her.

Janice walked back into the kitchen and slid onto the stool. Her expression had changed.

"Everything okay?" Carolina asked.

"You know I don't talk about my private business." Janice's lip quivered.

Carolina frowned. "I wasn't trying to snoop. Just making sure you were okay." She wasn't without compassion.

"That was Chris. He said he isn't coming home. Not until his honeymoon is over."

Carolina cocked her head. "You thought he'd come back because you're here?"

"Of course. I am his mother. He's my only child. He should come back when I need him."

"I'm sure you'll see him soon enough. It's only a few more weeks."

"I don't have a few more weeks." Janice blinked. "I'll be on a cruise by the time he gets back."

Carolina rolled her eyes. She turned back around and concentrated on the chili.

"Aren't you going to ask about Chris?"

"No. We are no longer married. What he does is his business." She reached down and petted Phoenix on top of the head and secretly wished the dog could turn into a dragon and chase her ex-mother-in-law out of the house.

"It's almost eleven at night there. I'm surprised he's still up that late. But I guess with a younger woman he feels younger too. He said they went to the Louvre today. I went to Paris a few years ago with some friends. Had a wonderful time. Have you ever been?"

"You know I haven't." She stated.

"He sounded tired when we spoke." Janice said as she walked over to the fireplace.

"Probably because he's trying to keep up with a twenty-two year-old." She muttered under her breath.

"He said they are planning on going to Greece after Paris."

"Do you want peppers in your chili?" She didn't have any peppers but desperately wanted to change the subject.

"You know I can't tolerate them." Janice pressed her

lips into a thin line. "He said the weather is wonderful over there. And I could tell he was sad about missing my trip to his house."

She snorted. Chris Johnson was the most self-entitled man she'd ever met. He was probably glad he missed the visit with his mom. Whenever she visited, he made sure to take calls so he wouldn't have to be around her.

"Dinner will be ready in about an hour." She put the lid on the pot and let the ingredients simmer. "I'm going to have a hot tea and sit outside. Would you like one?"

"I'll take a tea but I refuse to sit out there in this cold weather."

Carolina bit back a sharp reply and instead fixed two cups of hot tea and handed one to Janice. She took hers and gathered her jacket. Phoenix was on her heels following her to the back door.

Once outside she sat down in the chair and enjoyed her tea in peace with Phoenix at her feet.

The door swung open and her heart sank.

"Aren't you going to ask about Chris and his new wife?"

Carolina set her cup down on the table. "Janice why are you here? I mean you have made it abundantly clear that you have never liked me or thought I was good enough for your son. Now that I'm out of his life and yours, you are still here? Have you not tormented me enough?"

CHAPTER 30

*C*arolina stared as Janice blinked and then opened her mouth to say something. When she couldn't find the words she slammed her lips shut and stormed back inside.

Carolina sat there unmoving. Her heart was beating like a rabbit in her chest.

She couldn't believe she'd just spoken to her ex-mother-in-law like that, not when she'd been taught better by her mother. Carolina had always treated Janice with kindness even when Janice had been emotionally cruel.

All those years of shoving down her emotions had come out when she fell victim to Janice's verbal attack.

With trembling hands she reached for her tea.

Phoenix laid his head on her thigh as if sensing her emotions.

She smiled and rubbed his head, glad for his compassion.

Guilt suddenly seeped into her chest. Her mother wouldn't have approved of what she'd said.

"Love your enemies, bless those who curse you, do good to those who hate you and pray for those who mistreat you and persecute you. ~Matthew 5:44 "

She could almost hear her mother's voice as she read the Bible scripture.

No matter what had happened between her and Chris, she shouldn't have spoken to Janice that way. Even if Janice deserved it.

She stood and gathered her teacup. As much as she hated to go inside she knew she must.

Her mother raised her right.

She missed her mom so much in that moment, her chest felt like it would explode with grief.

She needed her now, more than ever.

Swallowing her pain she opened the back door and stepped inside.

Janice was nowhere in sight.

Phoenix peered around her legs making sure the coast was clear before coming inside.

She couldn't blame the animal.

Carolina put her teacup into the sink and walked toward the guest room. The door was closed. She knocked on the door. "Janice?"

No answer.

Carolina tried the lock. The knob wouldn't budge.

"Janice, I need to talk to you."

No answer.

Carolina sighed feeling terribly about the words she

said. But she knew Janice. Once offended she could hold a grudge like nobody's business.

Shaking her head Carolina headed into the kitchen. The aroma of chili filled the air. She lifted the lid and stirred the ingredients.

Carolina was tired. In her body and in her soul and in her heart.

She didn't have the energy to even eat the meal she'd made.

Finding a large glass container with a lid, she scooped the chili into the bowl to put into the refrigerator. She would have it for dinner tomorrow.

Carolina fed Phoenix, whose appetite had not been affected by the day's events.

"Wish I could live like you buddy."

Carolina stayed outside letting Phoenix do his business after his dinner and before heading to bed.

She wanted to knock on Janice's door again but she didn't. There was no place for Janice to sleep, and she would eventually end up on the couch.

Carolina went into the linen closet and pulled out a pillow and blanket and placed them both on the couch.

When Janice was ready for bed she would have someplace to lay her head.

Carolina could offer her that much at least.

CHAPTER 31

*C*arolina woke up before the alarm on her phone went off. She padded to the bathroom to get ready for the day.

After she'd showered and dressed, she headed into the kitchen. Phoenix had followed her into the kitchen while she made coffee. Carolina had been so tired she neglected to prep the coffee the night before.

When she was done she headed to the back door and spotted Janice asleep on the couch.

Janice had her hands under her cheek as she slept, her mouth slightly ajar.

She looked vulnerable. More vulnerable than Carolina had ever seen.

She walked over and pulled the blanket up over her shoulders before turning her attention to taking Phoenix outside.

Stepping out into the cold air, she walked down the

stairs toward the lake. Phoenix followed. She wrapped her arms around her as she watched the wind play on the waves of the water. The sun was trying to peek over the water.

She breathed in deep, the air burning her lungs.

"Good morning."

She spun around shocked to see Janice behind her.

"Good morning. I didn't expect you to get up so early."

"I didn't sleep very well," Janice huffed.

"I'm sorry." She took a drink of her coffee.

"Maybe today you can go buy a proper mattress for that bed."

"Janice, I've got to be at work in an hour. And even if I didn't have to work, I don't have the extra money for a mattress."

"That's crazy. Of course, you have the money. You got half of all my son's hard-earned assets. Everyone knows the wife of a husband as well-off as Chris has to give the ex-wife substantial funds."

"I wish he had. But unfortunately, all I got in the divorce was this lake house and a paltry alimony for three years." She shrugged.

"I don't believe that. You just don't want me here."

"Janice I don't have the energy to argue with you. Ask your son." She shook her head and walked past her.

Janice said something but she didn't hear her. The words were white noise in her ears.

Phoenix noticed the danger of the older woman, and didn't leave Carolina's side. When she stepped inside the house Phoenix was right beside her.

CHAPTER 32

"You have a phone call." Bernice glared at her.

Carolina stood up from arranging pumpkins around some haystacks and mums. "Me?"

"Yeah you." Bernice yelled. "This ain't no dating line so hurry up." She shoved the phone at Carolina.

"Hello?"

"Carolina."

"Thomas? What's wrong?" He had never called before. From the tone in his voice she knew it was something serious.

"It's your ex-mother-in-law."

She cringed. "Is she still there?"

"Yeah, and she won't let me do my job."

"What do you mean? Just get up on the roof and ignore her."

"She won't let me near my ladder," he said.

"You're kidding me."

"Do I sound like a man who kids?"

"No. You sound like a man who has never laughed a day in your life," she admitted.

He snorted. "Want me to call the cops?" I'm trying to get your roof finished and she isn't helping my progress."

"No. I'll take an early lunch and deal with her." She ended the call and looked over at Bernice who was staring at her.

"That was Thomas."

"I know."

"He said my ex-mother-in-law won't let him put my roof on."

"Tell him to ignore her."

"I did. From the sounds of it, she's literally blocking his ladder."

"If you leave, you are taking it as your lunch break." Bernice narrowed her eyes.

"Fine." Carolina grabbed her purse from behind the counter and hurried to her car.

By the time she pulled into her driveway she saw Janice leaning against the ladder, blocking the only way for Thomas to get on the roof.

"What's going on here?" Carolina demanded. "Thomas needs to get back on the roof so he can fix it."

"I'm not moving. I asked to see this man's credentials. I believe a roofer needs some kind of license. Therefore I'm stopping work until I'm satisfied that my son's house is in good hands."

Incensed, Carolina stepped forward. "Yeah, well, it's

not your house, it's mine and if you don't move, I'm going to call the police."

"You have got to be kidding me." Janice glared at her.

"Try me." The words spilled out of her mouth.

Phoenix arrived, saw the interaction, and stood over by Thomas unsure of what was going on.

When Janice didn't move, Carolina dug out her cell phone. She began punching in numbers.

Janice tried to call her bluff.

"Yes, can you send a police officer out to my house? I have a crazy woman who is trespassing on my property and won't leave." She proceeded to give her the address.

"Carolina Johnson! How dare you." Janice thundered. She stood from perching on the ladder and fisted her fingers at her sides. "I cannot believe you called the police on me like I'm a common criminal."

"You really called the cops on her?" Thomas arched his brow.

She ignored his question and kept her gaze on Janice. "They are on their way so you can either wait here and take it up with the police or you can leave."

Janice smugly crossed her arms and glared. "We'll see what they have to say."

Off in the distance the wail of a siren was heard.

Carolina gasped.

Janice's smile slid off her face. Her face went pale. "You actually called the cops on me." She ran inside.

"Huh." Thomas snorted, unable to hide the fact he was impressed.

It took less than thirty seconds for Janice to come barreling out of the house with her suitcase and belongings.

She threw them in the car and got behind the wheel. She started the engine and peeled out down the driveway.

"I've never seen her move that fast." Carolina stared after her. "She always said she had a bad hip."

"She looked fine to me. I can't believe you called the cops on her."

"I actually didn't." She looked up at him. "I called Bernice."

A familiar car pulled into the driveway. Bernice rolled down the window and looked between the two of them. "Is she gone?"

"Yes, but when I called you I was calling her bluff. I didn't mean for you to call the cops."

"I didn't call the cops." She sneered. "I tripped my house alarm. I knew they would send a police car out. The siren you heard was them at my house."

"That's actually brilliant," Carolina smiled.

"What would be more brilliant is you getting back to work. I had three people who live on the lake come by after you left. They said they saw your front door and were asking if we could do something like that for them."

She brightened. "See I told you it would bring in business."

"Good thing too. You still owe me for my vet bill."

"I know, I know." She looked at Thomas. "Everything okay here?"

"Yeah. Next time I get a crazy lady I can't handle I will definitely call you." He grinned.

Driving back to work, Carolina couldn't help but feel she'd won a major battle that day.

She had never measured up when it came to her ex-mother-in-law. But today, she'd at least earned her respect. Janice would never cross her again.

But that was all in the past.

And now she could focus on looking toward her future.

CHAPTER 33

*I*t was Sunday and she had the day off. She spent it by sleeping in until seven and enjoying her cup of coffee on the back deck with Phoenix.

"Hello? Is anyone home?"

She jumped in her seat. "Yes?" She stood and Phoenix barked at the woman coming from around the front of the house. The woman was around her same age and was very attractive with blond hair and blue eyes. In her youth she would have been stunning.

"I tried knocking but no one answered." She cast a worried look at Phoenix. "Does he bite?"

"He hasn't yet." She tightened the belt on her robe and crossed her arms over her chest. "Can I help you?"

"Yeah, Bernice told me you're the owner of this house. My name is Hannah Reece. I live next door."

"I'm Carolina Johnson, nice to meet you." She smiled.

"I've been trying to contact the owner for months trying to get compensated for the damage to my mailbox that your renters caused." Hannah eyed her suspiciously.

"I heard about that when I arrived." Her own smile slipped.

"You didn't know about the damage when it occurred?" Hannah cocked her head like she didn't believe her.

"No I didn't. You see my husband, I mean my ex-husband, rented the lake house out and took care of all of that. I never knew anything about it. He kept me away from that kind of information. He kept me away from a lot of things." She sighed. "Anyway, I got the lake house in the divorce. Along with all the issues." She held up a finger. "Let's go inside so I can write down all your information."

Hannah nodded slowly and walked up the steps and into the house.

"Would you like some coffee?" Carolina pulled out a pen and pad from a kitchen drawer. She refilled her coffee cup and looked over at Hannah.

"Thank you. That would be nice." Hannah didn't smile but sat at the kitchen island. There was a sadness behind her eyes.

She quickly made a cup of coffee for Hannah and set the cream and sugar by her cup.

"I'm sorry I haven't been over to your house to compensate you. I've been busy trying to get a new roof on my house."

"I saw Thomas's truck over here. He does good work." Hannah took a sip of her coffee.

"Good. For what I'm paying him, he better." She chortled.

Hannah gave her a slight smile.

"I bet your husband was pretty mad about the mailbox. My ex would have been livid." Carolina shoved the pen and pad toward her. "If you'll just tell me your address, I can get someone out there to fix it as soon as I get the roof on… and pay Bernice's vet bill…" She bit her lip. "I have to confess it may be a while before I can afford it, but I promise I will pay to have it fixed."

"Oh it's already fixed. James fixed it himself before…" She looked away.

She recognized the look in Hannah's eyes. She'd seen it in her own reflection. "Oh my gosh." She lowered her voice. "Your husband didn't leave you too did he?"

The woman sitting in her kitchen slowly nodded. "He did."

"I'm so sorry. I understand how that feels. I can't believe a man would leave you. I mean, I'm in my forties and no longer a spring chicken. I knew I had put on some weight but I was trying to get it off. It didn't matter. He found what he was looking for in a twenty-two year old. But I mean look at you, you're gorgeous. I can't imagine any man leaving you."

Hannah looked at her and grimaced. "Carolina, my husband didn't divorce me. He died."

CHAPTER 34

*C*arolina's mouth dropped.

"Oh Hannah. I'm so sorry. I had no idea."

"How could you? You just moved here." Hannah stood and walked over to the fireplace. "Have you lit it yet?"

"No. Thomas was going to check it out to make sure it was in proper working order before I made a fire." She followed her into the living room.

"Maybe I need to ask Thomas to look at mine. I forget how many things James took care of. Now that it's just me, I have a lot more to do."

Carolina was unsure what to say. She barely knew this woman, yet it seemed they had so much in common."Do you have children?" she asked.

"Yes. A boy and a girl." Hannah laughed a little. "Of course they are grown now. Ella lives in Atlanta where she works and Gregory lives in Charlotte with his wife."

"How long have you lived on the lake?"

"We built out here while the kids were still in school." She smiled wistfully. "We would spend every weekend out here and when the kids went off to college, we sold our home in Charlotte and moved out here permanently."

"I bet you two shared some wonderful memories out here."

"We did." Her smile faded. "Now that it's just me in that big house it feels kind of lonely."

"Your kids come to visit, don't they?"

"Right after James died they did. But they have their own lives and are busy. I'm not even sure I'll see them on Thanksgiving."

"Well, it will just be me here at Thanksgiving so you're welcome to come over."

"You don't even know me." Hannah cocked her head.

"I know. But I also know what it's like to be lonely. And considering I kicked my former mother-in-law out yesterday, I'm kind of short on guests for the holidays."

Hannah looked at her. "You kicked your mother-in-law out?"

"Well yeah." She bit her lip. "I kind of feel bad about it."

Hannah burst out laughing. Carolina joined in. Even Phoenix, wanting to be part of the group started howling.

When the laughter and the howling died down, Carolina wiped the tears from her eyes.

"Thanks for the offer. I'll keep it in mind." Hannah glanced at her watch. "I need to be going."

"Wait. You didn't write down your phone number or how much it cost for the mailbox." Carolina held out the pen and paper.

Hannah hesitated and finally took it. She scribbled something down and handed it back to her.

Carolina glanced down and frowned. "But you only wrote down your phone number. You didn't tell me how much I owe you for the mailbox."

Hannah reached for the door leading out to the deck. She looked over her shoulder. "You don't owe me anything. I didn't really expect to get paid. I was just curious about the new neighbor. Besides, I haven't laughed like that in a while." She walked out the back door and back to her house.

CHAPTER 35

She spent the morning reading her Bible over a cup of coffee. When she was done she decided to try out the new leash she'd bought for Phoenix. She'd been there over a week and had yet to check out the whole neighborhood, so she decided to take the dog for a walk.

After changing into some yoga pants and a light jacket and sneakers, she started off.

When she reached the end of her driveway, she glanced back at the house.

The new roof was going to look good against the red siding. Her flowerbeds were popping with color and the mums were rallying despite Bernice's doubts. The décor near the door looked really cute. Her mind was already spinning with new ideas for a Christmas theme.

Smiling with satisfaction, she started off down the road.

She passed Hannah's house and slowed her strides so she could take it all in.

While her own red lake house was quaint, Hannah's house was a mansion.

The two-story luxurious log cabin looked like it belonged on the ranch of a Wyoming cattle baron. Large beams and stone accentuated the front with large picture windows. Carolina could only imagine what the inside looked like.

No wonder Hannah felt so alone in the house. It was massive.

She continued her walk looking at all the different homes on the lake. Some were single stories while others were massive two-stories like Hannah's.

She passed Bernice's house and stopped to admire the woman's house.

It was an older single-story home with dark-green siding and red-windows framing. It had a front porch with a swing and a few plants along the steps leading up to the house.

The place was certainly charming and it totally did not suit Bernice.

"She could use some fall décor on her porch," she muttered aloud. She looked down at Phoenix. "How mad will she be if I took some items from her nursery and arranged them on the porch?"

Phoenix whined.

"You're probably right. I'll have to think about it before I dare move forward with that decision." She urged the dog on and they continued their walk.

The house next to Bernice's was a newer model house. It was painted a cute shade of yellow with flower boxes in the window and a large porch with wicker furniture.

She could imagine a retired couple drinking coffee on that porch and reading the newspaper.

The idea caused something to twinge in her chest.

She never really thought about the future when she was with Chris. It was like she was just barely hanging on, day by day, to see if he would wake up to the fact he'd married beneath him and leave.

In the end, that's exactly what had happened.

She'd spent so much time worrying that she forgot about living.

Carolina continued walking, so caught up in her thoughts, that she didn't see the child on the bicycle until it was too late.

The child raced full speed down the driveway and crashed straight into Carolina. Both went tumbling onto the ground.

Pain ricocheted through her body as she lay on the cold asphalt. Phoenix was at her side licking her face and whining. "I'm okay, boy." She pushed herself up on her elbows.

A sharp pain shot straight through her leg.

Carolina glanced over at the young boy on the bicycle scrambling to his feet. He couldn't be more than eight years old. He spotted her and went wide-eyed. Without a word, the kid grabbed his bike and sped away leaving her on the ground.

"Oh my gosh." A woman came running down the driveway. She knelt beside Carolina. "Are you okay?"

"I think so." She got to her feet with some assistance. "Nothing seems to be broken so that's good." She gave a wry smile. "I'm sorry. I should have been paying attention."

"Sorry? Don't you be sorry for anything. I have warned him about darting out on the road like that. He never listens to me." She narrowed her eyes in the direction he'd taken off.

"Are you his mother?" If she was, she was pretty young.

"No. I'm his sister. My name is Sarah Williams. Our parents passed and I'm his guardian now." Sarah held out her hand.

"Oh I'm sorry to hear that." Carolina brushed the dirt off her hand and shook it. "I'm Carolina Johnson by the way. I am the owner of the house a few houses back. The one with red siding." She shrugged.

"Oh I know the one…the house with the pretty fall décor outside." She crossed her arms over her chest. "It looks great. I love what you've done. I admire that you used an old watering can for décor."

"I found it at a yard sale. Got it for next to nothing."

She sighed. "I don't have time for things like that anymore. But I used to love to go to garage sales and find something old, usually furniture and make it into something new."

"Wow. I bet that takes talent. I'm more of a green

thumb. I'm working at Bernice's nursery. That's where all the flowers and pumpkins came from."

"I wonder if Johnny would like to go pick out a pumpkin. Our parents used to do those things all the time, but we don't seem to have much time for things like that anymore." She shielded her eyes against the brilliant sun and looked for the boy.

"Well, if you change your mind drop by anytime. And I would appreciate it if you mentioned that Bernice's nursery is decorating porches for fall and Christmas this year. I could use the business."

"Of course. It's the least I can do since my idiot brother ran you down." She spotted Phoenix and smiled. "What a cute dog."

"Thanks, his name is Phoenix." She looked down at him. "He's friendly if you want to pet him."

She bent and held out her hand. Phoenix sniffed and then lowered his head so she could pet him.

"He's a sweet boy." Sarah stood.

"He just showed up at my house. No one has claimed him so I guess he's mine."

"I used to volunteer at the animal shelter and we got a lot of animals that had been abandoned. It's sad. But at least he has a good home with you."

"Thanks. I certainly have appreciated his company."

"I need to go get Johnny. Welcome to the neighborhood." She waved and headed back to the house to get her car.

"Thanks." Carolina called after her.

CHAPTER 36

"What did you do this weekend?" Bernice came up and crossed her arms across her chest.

"Nothing exciting." Carolina stacked another pumpkin on the wagon in front of the nursery.

"Because I've had calls this morning asking how much it would cost to decorate their porch and front door. They said they saw your front door and want something like that for theirs. They're also asking to be put on the list for Christmas decorating."

Carolina clasped her hands together with delight. "That's wonderful! That will certainly drum up business for you."

Bernice fisted her hands at her sides. "I have no idea how to decorate peoples' porches. I'm in the nursery business not the décor business."

"Just give it a chance. It seems like there is a demand

so you can price it whatever you want. Besides I'll do the decorating." Carolina smiled.

Bernice snorted. "People aren't going to want to pay what I want to charge."

"I bet you'll be surprised," Carolina challenged.

A car pulled up and both women turned their attention to the customer. To Carolina's surprise it was Hannah.

"Hi, Hannah." Carolina greeted her.

"Hello Carolina, hello Bernice." She walked toward them wearing jeans and a cream colored sweater paired with a long pair of black leather boots. She had her blonde hair pulled back in a messy bun and silver earrings dangled from her ears. She looked like she stepped off the cover of a travel magazine.

"What can I do for you today? Want some mums for your house?" Bernice pointed at the flowers.

"I wanted to come by and get some ideas for my front porch. I saw the wonderful job that Carolina had done with hers and I want to give it a shot."

"That's great. You have a wonderful entryway and porch so you'll need a lot of mums and accessories." Carolina pulled out her phone. "I have some ideas here that you might like." She pulled up her Pinterest page and turned the phone where she could see.

"I love this one. And of course I'll need some for my back deck and outdoor living area as well." She glanced at her car. "I don't think it will all fit in my car."

"We can deliver to you." Carolina offered.

"We can?" Bernice gave her a weird look.

"Sure. Now let's pick out the colors you want, and we have a few ferns left over that would look great as well. They are discounted so you're getting a deal on those." Carolina walked Hannah over to the greenhouses and spent the next thirty minutes discussing ideas. By the time she left she'd spent a great deal of money.

"See, it's already paying off. You made more on that sale than what you made all week." She showed her the bill of sale.

"Yeah. And how do you suppose we get all that over to her house? Between your jeep and my car it still won't fit."

"Perhaps Thomas would let me borrow his truck."

"Not likely. He had to take Stanley to his doctor's appointment. I saw them at the diner this morning."

"Hmm. Well let me think." If nothing else she could rent a truck for the day. "I wonder if I call Freddy how much he'd charge for delivery. I bet he'll do it for a low fee."

"There's another customer. You go talk to them while I finish watering the mums. I'll call Freddy and confirm with him about delivery." Bernice grabbed the water hose and headed in the direction of the greenhouse.

Carolina watched a young couple get out of their SUV with two kids in tow.

"Welcome. Can I help you find something?" Carolina smiled.

"Yes, we were wondering if you had any experience with decorating a porch for the fall?"

Carolina smiled and looked over her shoulder. Bernice was rolling her eyes at Carolina.

"Yes of course. Just follow me and we can get you all set up.

CHAPTER 37

*C*arolina had just finished drying her hair when her cell phone rang. She frowned at the unknown number but answered it anyway.

"Hello?"

"Carolina, it's Rebecca. From the bank."

She immediately brightened when she recognized her friend's voice. "Oh yes, hello. How are you?"

"I'm fine but I'm afraid there's an issue and I need you to come down to the bank today."

"Okay I guess I'll tell Bernice I'll be a little late. She's not going to like it."

"This is important."

"Okay. I"ll be there at eight." She hung up and quickly dialed Bernice's number.

She explained the situation and Bernice told her she was going to have to work late to make up her hours.

She grabbed a cup of coffee and let Phoenix out for

the day. She spotted Thomas putting his ladder up against the roof.

"Good morning." He waved.

"Good morning." She glanced at the time, making sure she wasn't going to be late for her meeting with Rebecca. "Would you like some coffee?"

"Sounds good." He dusted off his hands against his pants and headed up the deck to where she was standing.

He followed her into the kitchen. "How is Stanley?"

"He's good. He's got half the widow women from the church waiting on him hand and foot. If this keeps up I'll never get him back to work." He grinned and then sobered. "Everything okay? You look worried."

"I just got a call from Rebecca at the bank. She said I need to come in as soon as the bank opens. I hope there's nothing wrong with the loan."

"They already approved you for the loan. They probably just want you to sign some more papers. Banks are always like that."

She nodded. "You're probably right. I'm just worrying for nothing." She didn't mention the urgency of the call, or that Rebecca said it was important enough for her to have to go to work late.

She glanced at the time on her phone. "I guess I should get going. There is some left over chili in the refrigerator if you get hungry. I'm locking the front door but feel free to come in through the back."

"If I leave before you get home I'll lock up."

"Thank you." She smiled and rinsed off her coffee

cup and set it in the sink. She grabbed her purse and headed over to the bank.

On the drive over there she tried to rack her brain as to why Rebecca wanted to see her.

After all, she'd already gotten the loan, secured a job for herself, and was putting equity back in the house with a new roof.

Had something happened? Were they revoking the loan? Could they even do that?

As she turned down the street to the bank her heart raced.

CHAPTER 38

She walked into the bank and headed for Rebecca's desk. She looked up from typing on the computer.

"Carolina, thank you for coming in so fast."

"It sounded urgent."

"Please sit." Rebecca waved her into the chair across from her desk. "How's the roof coming?"

"It's coming. Thomas is putting the shingles on now. He has to get a second load in tomorrow to finish everything so I'll have to give him another check for that."

"I see." Rebecca nodded and hit some keys on the keyboard. They were becoming friends, so why was her expression anything but friendly? In fact, she looked very serious.

Carolina fidgeted with the clasp on her watch, trying to ignore how clammy she felt or the fact her heart was racing in the same manner it had in the attorney's office that day. She swallowed.

"What's wrong?"

"Well when you took out the loan it was specifically for a new roof. That means the line of credit is only supposed to go for anything to do with the roof. Like shingles, labor, etc."

Carolina nodded. "I know."

Rebecca folded her hands in front of her on the desk. "Carolina I know this must be a difficult time for you. Newly divorced and figuring out how to live and what to do. But when you signed for the line of credit it meant the money could not be used for anything else."

"I know. And that's all I've done with the money. Rebecca what exactly are you saying?"

Rebecca cocked her head. "Have you used the funds for the line of credit on anything else? Say a new mattress and bedroom suite at Second Hand Furniture in town?"

"No. I only used the funds for the roof."

"Actually you're the one who paid for it."

"What?" Carolina's heart thumped like a two-year-old pounding on a drum. "I—I don't understand. There must be a mistake."

"I noticed a check was written out of the line of credit account and it was made out to the furniture place. When I called and asked about it, they said an older woman came in and bought a new bedroom suite and mattress. It was the most expensive bedroom suite they had. It was around five thousand dollars."

Nausea washed over her. "Oh my gosh."

"When I asked the manager to describe the woman, the description didn't match you." Rebecca tapped her pen on her desk. "Carolina, it sounds like your ex-mother-in-law is the one who forged a check in your name. From the look on your face, you had no knowledge of it."

"I can't believe my ex-mother-in-law did this to me." She looked at Rebecca. "What does this mean?"

"It means you can press charges. Since she literally stole your checks."

"What about the roof?"

"About that. You'll still have to pay the entire loan off and because she used your funds, you are now five thousand short to pay Thomas. We can rectify this but it will take some time."

"Time is not something I have." She buried her face in her hands. "I can't believe this."

"Carolina I'm so sorry. The bank has every legal standing to press charges against Janice for fraud. But since we are a small town, we may not have to get the authorities involved. I wanted to speak to you first. If she pays everything back then we can fix this without legal intervention."

"I'm not even sure where she is. She left." Just when she was thought she was figuring out her life, this happens.

"So I need five thousand to finish the roof." She looked at Rebecca.

"That's right. I can try to see if the bank would be willing to extend the loan to cover what you need."

"No. Don't do that. I don't want to be in any further debt."

"Well, you could sell the lake house. If you think you're not able to keep it up. I know people are always looking for a lake house."

Where would I go? She said to herself. She straightened her shoulders and stood. "Thank you for letting me know about all this. I've got to get to work now. And figure out how to get five thousand dollars fast."

She walked out of the bank shoulders hunched and soul crushed.

CHAPTER 39

By the time Carolina got home, Thomas had already left for the day. Phoenix was waiting for her at the door, his tail thumping against the steps.

As she walked up to the door even the excitement of the dog couldn't put a smile on her face.

She opened the door and stepped inside. Her phone rang just as she put her purse on the kitchen island.

"Hello?"

"Carolina."

Her stomach dropped at the sound of Chris's voice.

"Carolina, are you there?"

"Yeah. What do you want?" She could barely keep a snarl from her voice. Like mother...like son. They had both done their best to ruin her life.

"I need to talk to you."

"Perfect. I need to talk to you."

"Carolina, the alimony check is going to be late."

"What?" Her stomach dropped a second time.

"Kylie wanted some renovations to the house and so your check is going to be late."

Anger surged in her veins threatening to spill to the top in a volcanic explosion of words.

"You are the most selfish person I've ever met. You aren't going to keep walking all over me."

"What's gotten into you? You used to be so accommodating."

"I guess I grew a backbone. If my check is late I'm going to let my attorney deal with it. Maybe being in contempt of a court order would do you some good."

"You would never…"

"Don't say never to me." She ended the call and collapsed on the couch.

She was tired. Tired in her body and tired in her soul. The kind of tired that sleep would never cure.

CHAPTER 40

"I can't believe my ex-mother-in-law did that." She sat back in the chair on the deck and looked out over the lake. She'd given Thomas a partial rundown of the story after he continued to ask her what was wrong when he showed up for work. She conveniently left out the part that Janice had used the line-of-credit check. He naturally assumed Janice had written a check on Carolina's personal account.

"I already called the furniture store that Janice bought the items from. They'll take it back but at a fraction of what she paid." She cut her eyes at him wondering if she should just come out and tell him she was going to be late paying him for the roof. Thomas was understanding. Surely he would work out a payment plan for her to finish paying for the roof. "Thomas, I was…"

His cell phone dinged.

He dug it out of his pocket and looked at the text. "Perfect." He groaned.

"What is it?"

"It's a reminder from the hospital that I have an appointment at noon."

"Hospital? Is everything okay?" She leaned forward and gave him her full attention.

"Oh it's nothing like that. I have to meet with billing to finish paying for Lilly's hospital bill. They are willing to settle the rest of the bill for a portion of what I owe if I pay them cash."

"Cash?"

"Yes. I've been paying the bill for so long that I went in to talk to them. I thought I would be paying on it until I died but since I got this job, I'm going to be able to finally pay it off." He settled back in the chair and gazed out at the lake.

Her mouth went dry. She nodded. "Well that's great."

"And it's thanks to you. You are the reason I'm able to do that. I know I've been hard to get along with but I appreciate that you hired me anyway." He gave her a little smile.

"I'm glad I could help," her voice was small and distant.

"A storm is coming through in two days. You need that roof on so I better get started." He stood and looked at her. "What are you going to do about your ex-mother-in-law? Any legal action?"

"I've already contacted my attorney. He's trying to

get in touch with Janice. He thinks she should pay the money back."

"You think she will?"

"I think she will if the attorney gets involved. She would be horrified if this all got out to her country-club friends."

"Ah, I see."

Carolina shook her head. "She never did like me. She never thought I was good enough for Chris."

He studied the lake in front of him. "You know I knew a lady like her once."

"You did?"

"Yeah. She had only one son. And when that son got married, she didn't like the daughter-in-law. But if you had known the mother-in-law's history you would know why."

That got her full attention.

"You see, the mother didn't get any kind of attention from the husband. He was successful and he was always at work. So, she poured all her attention and affection into her son. And when her son got married, she felt threatened. So she automatically didn't like the daughter-in-law."

"That's pretty sad."

"It is, once you see the whole picture." He looked into her eyes. "Did Janice ever bad-mouth her husband?"

"He had died when I came into the picture. But now that I think about it, yes. She did make little comments here and there about him."

"There you go. I guarantee with your ex-husband marrying this young girl, that's going to be a powder keg. Just imagine what Christmas will be like with that crew." He shuddered.

She laughed. "Thanks for cheering me up."

"Anytime. I need to get back to work."

She nodded and headed back inside.

She sank into the couch and sighed. It didn't look like there was much of a way out of this.

Her gaze landed on her mother's Bible on the coffee table.

She picked it up and thumbed through it. Her mother always told her the answers to all of life's problems could be found between these pages.

"If any of you lacks wisdom, let him ask God, who gives generously to all without reproach, and it will be given him." ~James 1:5

She sighed. "I'm trying God. I'm trying to hear what I'm supposed to do." She closed the Bible and reached for her purse. She pulled out her trusty pen and pad.

She wrote down her upcoming bills which included the electric and water. If needed, she could get by a week or two without groceries. She had a large box of oatmeal for breakfast and some frozen veggies that she could make a large pot of soup that would last a few days. She might have to do without creamer for her coffee but she could make it. The house was paid off so fortunately she wouldn't have a house payment.

Suddenly, an idea formed. The perfect solution to her inability to pay Thomas.

She twisted the wedding ring on her finger. She could sell her ring. Surely that would be enough money to pay for the rest of the roof.

She tugged the wedding band and ring off and set it on her Bible.

A twinge of grief washed over her. She was officially putting that large part of her life behind her, never to go back.

It had to be done. She had no other options.

She checked online to see what time the pawn shop opened. Thankfully it opened at seven. Plenty of time to go by there before going in to work.

CHAPTER 41

*C*arolina waited patiently for the jeweler to examine her diamond ring. It was at least two karats with diamonds around the band.

"Mrs. Johnson, how much were you wanting to get for the ring?" He frowned.

"Well, I know that it's two karats. Not counting the smaller diamonds, I think it should be worth at least ten thousand dollars. I checked online."

"The shape and cut for a diamond this size is worth quite a lot. You're right about that."

"That's great." She smiled.

"But there's a problem. This isn't a real diamond."

"Excuse me? Of course it's real. I've had it for almost twenty years."

He cringed. "Ma'am. It looks like your husband…"

"Ex-husband." She corrected.

"Yeah. It looks like your ex-husband gave you a cubic zirconia."

"But that's impossible. The ring belonged to his mother. He gave it to me when we got engaged."

"Hmmm. That would explain it."

"Explain what?"

"Well there are tiny marks on here which show the original diamonds have been replaced with fake ones." He gave her a sympathetic look. "I'm sorry."

"What?" She felt like she'd been hit in the stomach.

"I'm sorry to be the one to tell you, but this ring is basically worthless."

A brief second of hurt scraped across the expanse of her heart. It didn't last long. It was quickly drowned out by the wave of anger washing over her to the point she was seeing stars.

Her jerk of an ex was a truly pathetic person. How had she ever fallen in love with such a monster? Worse, how was she going to pay Thomas now?

"Ma'am, are you okay?" the man asked gently.

"Not really." She scooped up the rings and shoved them in her purse. "Thank you for your help."

"I'm sorry I couldn't be of more help."

She made her way outside and headed toward her jeep. Jennifer was standing outside her shop looking at her window display.

"Hey, Carolina. How are you doing?" She smiled brightly.

"Not well." She pressed her fingers to her temples.

"You look like you are about to faint. Come inside and sit for awhile." She gently grabbed her elbow.

"I can't. I've got to get to work."

"You can get to work after you come in and sit. I insist." She guided her inside the store and flipped the sign to Closed. She led her behind the counter and had her sit on the tall stool.

"Now sit here until I get some hot tea for you." She hurried to the back of the store. When she reappeared she was holding a hot cup of tea in a delicate white and yellow teacup.

She pressed it into Carolina's hands. "Drink this."

Carolina did as she was told.

"What's going on? Do I need to call anyone for you?"

"There's no one to call. It's just me." Tears stung the back of her eyes.

"Do you want to talk about it?" Jennifer asked gently.

"I'm a forty year-old divorced woman and I'm trying to start all over. My ex-mother-in-law who hates me, used my home equity loan to buy furniture for the guest room because she didn't want to sleep on the couch. I just found out and now I don't have enough money to finish my roof. And I have to pay Thomas because he's paying off his late wife's medical bills. I need the roof finished because there's a storm coming this week. So I went to the pawn shop this morning to pawn my engagement ring only to find out that the diamond I've worn for twenty years is fake. It belonged to my ex-mother-in-law. So now I'm at a loss as to where I'm going to come up with the money to pay Thomas. Oh, and my ex called and told me my alimony would be late because the new twenty-two-year old wife wants to redo a room in the house, probably in polka dots and rainbows. Did I tell you the new wife threw away my mother's quilt? The last quilt she made before she died." She swiped the tears pouring down her face. "I can't seem to get out of this pit I'm in, no matter how hard I try. It's like I'm standing in quicksand." Embarrased, she buried her face in her hands.

Jennifer pulled out a box of tissue and handed it to her.

"I'm sorry. I didn't mean to dump this all in your lap." She dabbed her eyes and blew her nose.

"Carolina, you can dump your problems on me anytime. That's what friends are for."

"Friends?" Carolina looked at her. "The last friends I had, knew about my husband's affair and never told me. I'm not sure I have ever really had a real friend."

"You do now." She smiled and patted her hand. "And I know Getty thinks the world of you. You have more friends than you know."

"Really?" Her sobs slowed.

"Yes really. Even Bernice likes you. But don't tell her I told you that. She likes to give people a hard time." Jennifer winked.

That drew a laugh out of Carolina.

"Now finish your tea and we'll figure something out." Jennifer patted her hand.

She did as Jennifer asked. By the time she finished her tea she was calm.

"I'm sorry. I didn't mean to say all that. I hope you don't think I'm crazy."

Jennifer barked out a laugh. "Honey we all have baggage. I'll have to tell you about mine sometime."

She glanced at the time on her phone. "Oh gosh. I need to get going. Bernice is going to chew me out for being late." She gathered her purse and headed for the door.

"If I can do anything let me know."

"I will, thanks. And thanks for the tea. And the shoulder to cry on."

"Anytime."

CHAPTER 42

"*W*hat's going on with you today?" Bernice glared over the pumpkins.

They'd been working the entire day selling pumpkins and mums to customers who wanted to do something different to their front porch. Every one of them had hired Carolina to decorate. Bernice was glad for the extra income but she certainly didn't show it.

"Nothing. Just busy." Carolina set a purple mum beside a grouping of pumpkins and some corn stalks.

"You've not smiled one time today. Not even when greeting the customers."

"So?"

"So? You always smile. You smile too much if you ask me." Bernice released and exaggerated huff and rolled her eyes.

"Then you shouldn't be complaining about it." Carolina snapped.

Bernice opened her mouth to say something, but two more cars of customers pulled in.

"Go wait on them." Bernice glared.

Carolina sighed and did as she was told. The first car just wanted to pick out some pumpkins so she told them to let her know if they needed anything.

Remembering Bernice's words, she pasted a fake smile on her face and walked up to the young man who had pulled up in a small economy car. She shook her head. There was no way he was getting anything in the backseat.

"Can I help you?"

"I hope so. My wife wants me to pick up some mums. For our front door. She didn't say what kind or what color. She said to make sure they would look good with our door and make sure to get plenty and make sure they were the right color." He grimaced.

"She should have come with you." She gave him a sympathetic smile.

"She would have but we have a newborn and she's been up with him at night. She wants to make this holiday perfect for the baby, but he won't even understand what's going on." He scrubbed his hand over his face. "I work nights at the hospital and I just got off. I don't want to mess up and get the wrong thing. Not to mention she won't put the baby in that car. I really need to get a bigger, safer car but I just haven't had time." He looked at his economy car.

"I understand. Let's see what we can do to make

your wife happy. You know we offer a decorating service."

"You do?" His eyes widened.

"Yes. Do you have a picture of your house so I can see the door?"

He nodded and flipped through some pictures. "I just painted the front door."

"Nice color." It was a dark navy against a light brick house.

"Thanks. My wife picked it out."

"You have a small stoop and no porch. I would suggest you decorate both sides of the steps leading up to the door in yellow and orange mums with pumpkins. I wouldn't even decorate the door. You don't want to overload it."

"Whatever you think. Can you give me a quote of how much it would cost for the supplies and how much it would cost for you to decorate it?"

"Sure. Let me do some quick calculations." She pulled a pencil and pad out of her small apron she wore as she worked. She looked at the picture and counted the steps. After calculating everything she handed him the scrap of paper.

"If this is what it costs to make my wife happy, then so be it." He looked at her. "And you will deliver?"

"Yes." She nodded. "I actually think I can get everything in the back of my jeep. I'll be over today if that's alright with you."

"That would be perfect." He smiled and relief slid

across his face. He pulled out a debit card and handed it to her. "Thank you so much."

"Of course. Just follow me inside and we'll get this rung up."

After he left she helped another customer with a sale.

"That makes five more houses to decorate." Bernice cocked her head. "Who knew people would be jumping on this like a duck on a June bug?"

She wanted to say that she did, but wisely held her tongue. She had enough problems as it was without making her boss mad at her. "I'll go over to the Clemson house today after work to get the house decorated."

"The Clemson house? Do you mean Tony and Katie Clemson?"

She frowned and read the name on the order. "Yes. You know them?"

"That's Hannah's nephew. I should have come over and spoken to them but I didn't recognize the car."

"I think he's in the market for a new one. He mentioned the wife doesn't want to put the baby in that car."

"Who can blame her? Why the whole thing looks like it would be totaled if it hit a squirrel." Bernice shook her head. "It's almost quitting time so just go on over there and start decorating their house."

"Are you sure?"

"Positive. I'll help you load up." Bernice had taken the order ticket and was heading over to the pumpkins.

CHAPTER 43

*C*arolina knocked on the front door of the Clemson's two-story house. It was tucked away on a quiet street in the middle of town. It was an older house and the perfect starter home for the new couple.

Tony answered the door on the first knock. He brightened when he saw her.

"Carolina, right?"

"Right. I got off early so I thought I would go ahead and get started."

"Thanks so much. And thanks for not ringing the doorbell. The baby is sleeping and so is my wife."

"Of course." She turned to head back to her jeep and then stopped. "You know, you should put a sign up on your door about not ringing the doorbell. And only knocking once."

"I hadn't even thought about that. But it's a good idea. Thanks."

She headed back to her jeep and opened the back.

"Wow. That's a lot of mums."

"Trust me, your wife will love it once she sees the finished product." They worked quickly to unload the jeep.

"Do you need me to do anything else?"

"No. I'll knock when I'm done so you can see it."

"Thank you." He went back inside and closed the door behind him.

She pulled up the picture of her inspiration she'd found on the internet and set it on the step. She began arranging the mums and pumpkins on either side of the steps. She'd also brought some burlap ribbon that they'd had lying in a corner of the nursery. She intertwined it between the mums and pumpkins and fluffed it where it needed it.

When she was finished she stepped back and admired her work.

Satisfied she knocked on the door.

Tony appeared with his wife holding their baby. "Carolina this is Katie. And baby Michael."

"Nice to meet you both." She smiled. "How sweet. He's beautiful." She said to Katie.

"Thank you." Katie gave her a tired smile. "Tony said you were going to make our house look more festive. I wish I had time to do it but there are only so many hours in the day."

"That's what I'm here for. I hope you like it." She stepped back and let the couple see her work.

Kate's smile dropped and she gasped. Tony was

looking at Katie. It occurred to Carolina that it didn't matter what it looked like to Tony, as long as his wife was happy, then he was happy.

"It's beautiful." Katie walked down the steps looking from side to side. "I thought you were going to put something up on the door and maybe a pumpkin and a mum, but this…" She blinked back tears. "This is amazing."

"I'm so glad you like it." Carolina smiled, feeling happy for the first time that day.

"I mean it. It's picture perfect." Katie shook her head in disbelief.

"So it is. Why don't I take some pictures of you? A family picture."

"But I don't have any makeup on." Katie touched her face.

"You look beautiful." Tony gazed at his wife.

"Run inside and get ready. I'll wait." Carolina nodded.

Katie hesitated for a minute and handed the sleeping baby to Tony. She hurried inside.

Tony gave Carolina a grateful smile. "Thanks for that."

"No problem. Decorating porches is what I do best."

"Not just that. For offering to take pictures. We had pictures planned for last week but Michael had colic so we canceled. She was so disappointed. She had outfits planned and everything."

"Really?" Well go change clothes." She looked down

at the baby. "I'll hold him while you both get changed if you want."

"Are you sure it's okay?"

"Of course." She held out her hands.

"Thanks so much." He placed Michael in her arms and hurried inside.

She stared down at the baby. He slept peacefully with his hands on either side of his face. She stared down at the sleeping babe and wondered what it would have been like to have a child. Would a son or daughter have changed the trajectory of her life? Would Chris still have left?

Not likely a child would have changed the situation. If fact, a child would have also been left in the wake of Chris' selfishness.

"Sorry that took so long." Katie came rushing out of the house. She held out her arms and Carolina handed the child back to her.

"Not a problem." She looked at Katie and Tony dressed in dark jeans and red sweaters. Katie tucked a red and black buffalo plaid scarf around Michael's body until he was swaddled.

"You guys will look great against the mums and pumpkins." Carolina nodded. "Where's your phone and I'll get some pictures."

"Here use mine." Tony handed her his phone. "Where should we stand?"

"Why don't we take some pictures with you guys at the top of the stairs and then some of you sitting on the steps?" Carolina nodded.

"Perfect." Katie smiled.

The couple posed while Carolina snapped some photos. She let Katie look at the photos to make sure she liked them before getting them to change to a different pose.

By the time she was done, she estimated that she'd taken close to thirty photos.

"I can't thank you enough." Katie smiled. "This means so much."

"I'm glad I could help."

"Once we get a bigger vehicle and we can get out of the house, I'm definitely coming to see you at the nursery." Katie looked at Tony.

"You don't happen to want to sell your Jeep do you?" Tony laughed.

"Only if you know someone willing to pay cash." She chortled.

"Are you serious?" Tony sobered. "Are you willing to sell your car?"

She blinked. Was she? "I am but I also need to get a car so I'll have a way to get to work."

"Mind if I look at your vehicle?" Tony cocked his head.

"Sure." She walked him over to the Jeep. "It's not new."

"I know but it's in good condition. And it's dependable. I've actually been looking at this model but it's hard to find." He slid into the driver's seat and took the keys she held out to him. He started the engine and looked at the mileage. "Mind if I look in the glove compartment?"

"Go ahead."

He pulled out the service schedule book and looked through it. He looked at the gauges on the dash and then slid out of the driver's seat. He popped the hood and examined everything. When he was done, he shut it and walked over to her.

"If you are serious about selling I have a suggestion for you."

"I'm listening."

"Your car is worth more than mine. I'll buy your car for five thousand dollars and I'll give you my car as well so you won't be out of a vehicle."

"Are you serious? You'll do that?"

"Yes. I've needed to get a bigger vehicle for a while but don't want a new car payment." He held out his hands. "I'm not trying to pressure you. It has to be your decision."

She nodded. "Can I let you know tomorrow?"

"Of course. You have my number from the order right?" He smiled and held out his hands.

"Yes, I do. I'll let you know for sure tomorrow."

"Again, I can't thank you enough for what you did for us. I haven't seen Katie smile like that in a while."

"It was my pleasure." She got into her Jeep and drove home.

CHAPTER 44

The next morning she headed into town after leaving the Clemson's house. She had business at the bank and she wanted it taken care of as soon as possible.

Rebecca stood from her desk as she got up. "Carolina, I'm glad you're here."

Carolina smiled. "Yes, I have some news. I have the money. She pulled out a check and showed it to her.

"I would ask if you robbed a bank but then I would know." Rebecca frowned. "How'd you get it?"

"I sold my vehicle."

"Oh, I wish you hadn't done that." Rebecca sank into her chair.

"It was a cash offer. The Clemsons' needed a car and I sold them mine."

"But what will you drive? You still need to be able to get to work." Rebecca looked concerned.

"I got Tony's car as well as cash for my Jeep."

"That little economy car?" Rebecca gave her a horrified look.

She laughed. "Yes. It gets me from one place to another and that's all that matters. And he says it's amazing on gas."

Rebecca chewed her lip. "There's something I wanted to talk with you about."

"Tell me Janice didn't write more checks on my name." She narrowed her eyes.

"Oh no. Nothing like that. But I would like you to step into the conference room."

"Okay." She followed her into the room with a large table. Standing at the end of the table was a woman with her back to her.

"If everyone will sit." Rebecca sat at the head of the table and motioned for Carolina to sit beside her.

The woman turned around and Carolina gasped.

"Janice. What are you doing here?" Carolina stared.

"She's here because I called in a favor to a state trooper friend of mine. What she did was illegal. He found her and had her escorted back here."

"I cannot believe you called the police on me like a common criminal." Janice fisted her hands at her sides.

"Janice Johnson. You need to sit down." Rebecca demanded.

Rebecca had always been kind to Carolina but it was clear that she had had enough of Janice.

"If you prefer not to sit then I can call the police in here to escort you to a jail cell where you might be more comfortable."

Janice's eyes popped but she did as Rebecca said and sat across from Carolina.

"We are here because we are straightening some things out." The phone on the table rang and Rebecca answered it. "Perfect. Put him through."

"Hello?" A male voice sounded confused on the speaker.

"Mr. Johnson. This is Rebecca with the bank. I have your mother Janice and your ex-wife Carolina sitting in the conference room with me. Mr. Johnson, a crime has been committed and I think you need to hear what's going on."

"What's the meaning of this? I'm in Paris. We are about to head to Greece."

"It can wait. And if you hang up on me there will be legal ramifications."

Chris was silent for a minute before he muttered. "Fine. But can you make it quick?"

"You need to know that your ex-wife secured a line of credit with our bank because the lake house that she got in the divorce was in dire need of a roof."

"So? What's that got to do with me?"

"Well, it appears your mother stole Carolina's checkbook for the account of the line of credit, and went and bought some bedroom furniture since there was none in the lake house. It's a felony to forge some-one's name on a check."

Chris was silent.

"And after talking to Janice, it seems some more information has come to light."

"What are you talking about?" Carolina looked between the two women.

"It seems you, Chris, told your mother to get the checkbook and write the check. You told your mother to commit forgery."

"You what?" Carolina gaped at the phone. "Why would you do that?"

"It's not like that." He struggled to find the right words. "You've got to understand that she was constantly calling me on my honeymoon. I got tired of hearing her calling me and complaining. I might have mentioned to her to just buy some furniture. I didn't actually think she'd do it." Chris yelled.

Carolina looked at Janice who had gone pale. She felt a teensy bit bad for her, despite how Janice had treated her. Janice was still someone's mother.

"Why didn't you tell me that Chris told you to do that?" Carolina asked quietly.

"I honestly didn't think anything about it. He always made sure I was comfortable when I visited. Besides, he surely was going to pay it back once he was back in the States. I really didn't see the harm." She lifted her chin defiantly.

"So you thought it was okay to steal from Carolina?" Rebecca wrote something down on a legal pad.

"Well, I..." Janice stuttered.

"So that puts Carolina in a bind with her loan." Rebecca spoke to Chris.

"Not my problem." Chris countered.

"Your problem is that you have already told

Carolina you aren't paying her alimony on time. Which will now put you in breach of a court order and Carolina has every legal right to sue you. And, I for one am encouraging such action," Rebecca cooed.

"You can't do that." Janice shook her head. "If Carolina needs the money she should sell something." She looked down at Carolina's hand. "It looks like you already did. Where's your engagement ring and band?"

"My rings. I'm glad you noticed." Carolina cocked her head.

"You pawned them?" Janice narrowed her eyes.

"I tried but when the jeweler examined them he said they were worthless."

"That's a lie. I know for a fact that engagement ring is worth at least twenty-thousand dollars." Janice glared. "I told Chris to get that back from you in the divorce."

"Oh, the original diamond probably was. But the stones that were in there were replacements. The jeweler even said he saw the marks where the real diamonds had been taken out and replaced with fakes." She dug in her purse and pulled out the rings. She set them in front of Janice. "I have a feeling you already knew they were fake when you gave them to Chris to give to me."

Janice went pale and looked at the phone and shook her head. "That's not true. It can't be true."

"If you didn't change the stones then who did?" Carolina frowned.

"I think maybe Chris can help out with that." Rebecca sneered.

"Chris, did you know the stones had been changed?" Carolina stared at the phone.

Silence stretched in the room.

"Chris, now is the time to come clean." Rebecca nudged.

"You make it sound way worse than it is," Chris huffed.

"Did you take the diamonds out of the ring?" Carolina gasped.

"When we got engaged we didn't have much money and I needed a new car. So I changed out the diamonds."

Carolina narrowed her eyes. "You took the diamonds out to buy that two-seater convertible while you were in medical school?"

"Yeah. I needed that car."

"You already had a Toyota. You didn't need a convertible."

Janice kept silent through the interaction. She neither defended or accused her son. Carolina knew she wouldn't say a harsh word about him. No matter what he did.

"Is there anything else or can I go catch this flight to Greece?" Chris huffed.

"Oh, I think we have plenty of information from you. And let me warn you, Chris. If Carolina's alimony check is one day late you will be in breach of a court order. I know some very powerful attorneys who would love to fight this for Carolina. Keep that in mind." Rebecca ended the call before he could respond.

"I think you'll have your alimony check on time." Rebecca winked at Carolina. She stood. "I'll leave you two alone. And Carolina, I'm sorry you had to sell your car to get money for your roof." Rebecca glared at Janice.

Janice appeared shocked at that bit of information.

Once they were alone, Carolina spoke."I guess we are done."

"You sold your car?" Janice gasped.

"I had no choice. I was short on funds for my roof." She stood.

"Carolina, I have something to say. I don't understand how this all happened. Chris has always been a good boy, a good man."

She sighed. Janice was never going to change. She would defend Chris to her death.

"Janice, I wish you well. I hope you have a wonderful holiday with Chris and Kylie. I know you have next year to look forward to when you have a grand baby. Our relationship is officially over which should make you happy. I know it does me." She smiled politely and left the room. She spotted Rebecca in the corner where the coffee station was for employees. She made her way over.

"How did you do all this?" Carolina shook her head.

"I know you said you didn't want to press charges. But the more I thought about everything you went through, and how your ex-mother-in-law treated you,

I got angry. And then I decided to do something about it. So I took matters into my own hands."

"Do you really know some high-powered attorneys?"

"No. I was bluffing. And he fell for it."

"That's…amazing." A big smile broke out across her face.

"I am sorry you had to sell your car."

"Don't be. A great family has it and I was glad to help them out. Besides being in such a small car makes me feel younger." She laughed.

"Good. I'm glad something good came out of all of this."

"Me too." She sighed. "Now if you don't mind, I have to be going to work. I've got to get busy creating a new life."

She walked out of the bank feeling lighter than she had in years.

CHAPTER 45

"Here's the rest of your money." Carolina handed Thomas a check.

Thunder rolled in the back gound.

"You certainly have good timing." She smiled and looked up at the darkening clouds.

"Call it a gift. Also your fireplace is good to go. Feel free to build a fire in it." He smiled. "So what is your next project going to be?"

"I think the next thing on my list is to paint. I'm not a fan of the yellow and I want something cleaner, maybe a light gray."

"I've got a list of painters if you want to use them."

"Oh no." She shook her head. "I'm going to have to paint it myself. To save some money." She shrugged. "But if I take my time and work on it after work, I should be done by New Year's Day."

"You'll have plenty of time. It's not even Thanksgiving yet."

"Oh, speaking of Thanksgiving I was going to invite you and Stanley over to Thanksgiving dinner. I think Hannah and Sarah and her brother are coming. Bernice is even coming, if you can believe it. She said she would eat lunch with us and drop by her daughter's house afterwards. She says she'd rather miss all the drama that goes on over there. Getty has a family lunch but she'll be over after. Jennifer and Rebecca already had plans."

"What can I bring?"

"How about a side dish?"

"Green bean casserole?"

"Perfect. I'll see you then."

CHAPTER 46

*T*hanksgiving morning dawned bright and sunny. Outside Carolina's kitchen windows, the trees were holding fast to the last of the autumn leaves and the air smelled of woodsmoke burning in the houses that surrounded the lake.

Inside her guests all gathered around the two fold-out tables that Carolina had found for a deal at a garage sale. She'd covered them with a pretty tablecloth she'd picked up from Jennifer's shop and arranged some flowers in the middle.

She'd roasted the turkey and made dressing while everyone else brought side dishes and desserts. Honey corn, sweet potato casserole, green bean casserole, new potatoes, brusselsprouts, cranberry sauce, salad, and fresh homemade rolls lined the table. The kitchen island was laden with every kind of pie imaginable. Sweet potato pie, apple pie, chocolate chess pie, and lemon chiffon pie.

The fireplace was lit making the room feel warm and cozy.

"I've never seen so much food in my life." Sarah's brother Johnny's eyes lit up. He had apologized for running her over with his bike the second he came into the house. Carolina could tell that he was a good kid, just one that was missing his parents.

"Well I hope everyone is hungry. Thomas would you mind saying a blessing?" Carolina clasped her hands together.

"Sure."

Everyone bowed their heads as his deep voice echoed in the house while he thanked God for the food and the blessings of friendship. As he spoke, Carolina couldn't help but tear up at his words. She was grateful for the blessing of friendship in this season of her life. When she needed true friends, God had provided them.

"Amen." Everyone said in unison.

There was a knock at the door and Carolina went to answer it, surprised to see her new friend on the other side.

"Rebecca. What are you doing here?"

She shrugged. "My aunt and mom got into an argument over whose green bean casserole was better. It got ugly so I escaped and decided to come over here." Rebecca smirked. "And mom is kind of mad you didn't show up." She cut her eyes at Bernice, who shrugged like she didn't have a care in the world.

"Come on in. Glad to have you."

Everyone greeted her as she walked into the room. She stopped and turned to Carolina. "I also have a surprise for you."

"You do?"

"Yes. I received a package at the bank. It was from your ex-mother-in-law."

Everyone grew quiet.

"Really?" Carolina frowned.

"Yes. She sent a check for the amount that she took plus an additional amount. She said to deposit it into your account. And for you to use it to buy whatever you need for your house."

"What?" Carolina's mouth dropped. "Why would she do that?"

"Maybe it's her way of saying sorry for how she treated you all those years." Hannah shrugged. She had grown closer to Hannah over the weeks and they met regularly for coffee.

"You said there was a package?"

"Yeah." She held out a large gift bag.

Carolina took it and pulled out the tissue paper. She gasped. "It can't be."

"Oh it is." Rebecca smiled. "Janice said she found the quilt in a second-hand store in Charlotte. She recognized it and asked the owner of the shop where he got it from. He said some fool threw it in the garbage. He fished it out."

"It's my mother's quilt." Tears spilled out over her cheeks.

"God has a way of taking care of us in big and small ways." Rebecca smiled.

"I don't know what to say."

"Then don't say anything and come over here and eat." Thomas patted the chair beside him.

She sat down and looked around the table full of friends and realized just how blessed she truly was.

CHAPTER 47

*C*arolina pulled into her driveway after a long but satisfying day at work. Thomas's truck was parked in the front and Phoenix was nowhere to be seen.

She walked around to the backyard and spotted Thomas and the dog sitting on the porch.

"Hey, what are you doing here?" She smiled and stepped onto the deck.

"It seems weird not to come over here every day." He shrugged.

"Oh yeah. Did you miss me or was it Phoenix you couldn't wait to see?" She laughed.

"Both."

The smile nipped at the corners of her mouth and she ducked her head. She wasn't sure but she thought Thomas was flirting with her.

"Would you like something to drink?" She offered, hoping to prolong his visit.

"I would like for you to go for a walk down by the lake with me." Thomas stood and shoved his hand through his hair.

"Okay. Let me change into some sneakers." She unlocked the back door and headed to her room. She quickly changed her shoes and glanced at her reflection in the mirror.

She stopped.

Her short brown hair had grown out and was down around her shoulders. Her face was thinner, like the rest of her, and her brown eyes seemed to glow.

She debated putting on some makeup but since she'd moved to the lake house she'd not been wearing any. She shrugged and decided not to start now.

She ran a brush through her hair and headed outside.

Thomas was bent down patting Phoenix on the head. The dog had started to stick closer to home and not wandering off during the day. Maybe he realized his old family wasn't coming back and she was his family now.

She'd grown to love the dog and couldn't bear to think about being without him.

"I'm ready." She called out.

They walked down to the lake admiring the beautiful day.

"Are you still working on the grocery store roof?" She asked when they stopped at the water's edge.

"Yes, but I should be finishing up in a day or two.

Stanley is back on the job in a limited capacity so I feel like I'm babysitting him more than doing my job."

She grinned.

"How's the nursery business?"

"It's gearing back up for Christmas. I had no idea that Bernice was going to be selling full-size Christmas trees this year. She says she's never done that before but since we did so much business this past fall she wants to expand."

"Did you pay her vet bill yet?"

"I tried. With the money I got from Janice. But Bernice wouldn't take any money. She said she couldn't say for certain that Phoenix was the dog that bit her cat."

"I saw how she was loving on that dog at Thanksgiving. She knows as well as I do that Phoenix wouldn't hurt a fly." He chuckled.

"I'm just glad everything is going well."

They walked at a slow pace around the lake.

"What are you doing for Christmas?" He looked over at her.

"I'm not sure. Painting I guess."

"Would you like some company?"

"You want to spend your holiday painting?" She laughed.

"I just want to spend it with you. If I have to paint, so be it."

She sobered. "What?"

"Carolina, I know it's been a while since I've flirted

with a woman. Apparently, I'm doing a really bad job if you didn't realize I have feelings for you."

"For me?" Her eyes widened.

"Yes, you. And if I don't make my intentions known then some other guy is going to snatch you up. You're smart and beautiful and strong."

Her face broke into a smile. She had never heard those words from a man before.

"I know you don't want to rush into anything. I want us to take things slow."

Her heart skipped a beat. She would be taking a risk at getting her heart broken. But she couldn't live life in fear. Besides, Thomas was nothing like Chris.

She met his gaze. "I think I would like that."

"I came over here to ask you out on a date for Friday night. I'd like to take you out to dinner and then dancing."

"I haven't been dancing in forever."

"Then you're well overdue." He held out his hand. She put her hand in his. The warmth of his palm matched the warmth she saw in his eyes.

"Yeah I am." She smiled and gently squeezed his hand.

She turned and stared out across the lake.

She once thought her life was falling apart.

But in reality it was falling into place.

ABOUT THE AUTHOR

Jodi Allen Brice is an USA Today best-selling author of over thirty novels. She writes women's fiction and small town romance under Jodi Allen Brice and writes other genres under a different pen name. You can find her latest releases at http://jodiallenbrice.com

Harland Creek series

Promise Kept

Promise Made

Promise Forever

Christmas in Harland Creek

Promise of Grace

Promise of Hope

Promise of Love

Laurel Cove Series

Lakehouse Promises

Lakehouse Secrets

Lakehouse Dreams.

Harland Creek Mystery Quilters Series

The Mystery of the Tea Cup Quilt

The Mystery of the Drunkards Path